Deceptive Hearts

Marlene Chase

Annie's®
AnniesFiction.com

Books in the Amish Inn Mysteries series

Secrets of the Amish Diary
Plain Deception
Simple Lies
Murder Simply Played
To Love and to Vanish
Law & Old Order
A Silent Betrayal
Humble Pies and White Lies
Deceptive Hearts
Stolen Past
Grave Inheritance
Homespun Homicide
Broken Melody
Horse and Burglary
A Fatal Harvest
A Simple Deduction
The Hound and the Fury
Unhappy Returns
Skating the Law
Book Clubbed
Farmed Robbery
Scene of the Chime
Amish and Old Lace
To Honor and Betray

Library of Congress-in-Publication Data
Deceptive Hearts/ by Marlene Chase
p. cm.
I. Title
                    2016960063

AnniesFiction.com
(800) 282-6643
Amish Inn Mysteries™
Series Creator: Shari Lohner
Series Editor: Jane Haertel
Cover Illustrator: Kelley McMorris

10 11 12 13 14 | Printed in China | 9 8 7 6 5 4 3 2

Prologue

He paused at the entrance of the dimly lit café and watched the girl seated near the back. A smile tugged at his lips. She was as yet unaware of his presence. He hunkered down at the counter so he could watch her through the mirror above his head.

Of course she had come; he had only to smile at her, crook his little finger, and she came running. Women like her always did. Tell them they were beautiful, that you couldn't live without them, and they'd do anything for you.

He caught his sneer reflected in the mirror and worked to relax his lip. He needed her to do exactly what he said, so he must be his most charming and macho self. He'd found her appealing in the beginning, all soft curves and wide-eyed naïveté, fresh from some uptight religious family that kept her knitting mittens or peeling potatoes all day. He'd enjoyed showing her what she'd been missing in the big, wide world, but she was beginning to bore him.

He tilted his head to get a better view of his face with its five-o'clock shadow. He'd worked hard to get it looking just right—rugged but not too slummy. A sort of "Tom Hanks in the first part of *Castaway*" look. The jeans and satin-lapelled sport jacket over a white T-shirt reflected the confidence and success with which he wanted the world to see him. *Ah, you're a handsome dude*, he said to himself, viewing his square jaw, shiny black hair, and muscles hard enough to turn a girl's mind to mush. Though he was approaching forty, he prided himself on his youthful strength and the ability to capture the attention of women half his age.

He swiveled on the stool, stirring the drink a red-haired waitress had brought him, and fixed his eyes on the girl sitting pensively in the booth beyond. Bouncy curls the color of the winter sun surrounded a cherubic face with wide-set gray eyes, heavily lined with mascara. She was wearing the flowered tangerine-colored dress—his favorite. But she had topped it with a short white sweater, which to his mind covered too much of her excellent figure. He sighed. *You can take the girl out of the country but . . . If I could just keep the country out of the girl for a little while longer!*

He'd kept her waiting—not too long, but long enough so that she would still be eager to see him. He looked at her steadily until their eyes met and he was rewarded with a small pouty smile.

"Well, finally," she said, pushing her lips out in a scowl meant to rebuke him for his inattention. "How long have you been there watching me?"

He took her hands in his and leaned in close. "Not long," he said. *She's like a kid in a candy store*, he thought, noticing the eager glint in her eye as he held her gaze. He restrained a wry grin as he looked down at her fingers, each one sporting a sparkly ring. "I was just trying to imagine you quilting in front of the fire in your little white apron and *Kapp*."

She pulled her hands away and slumped back against the vinyl seat. "You're making fun of me again," she said, pushing out her lower lip. "You know it makes me mad." She folded her arms across her chest like a child in a fit of wounded feelings.

"But you're so cute when you're mad," he told her, cocking his head and smiling. He could see her softening and gave himself a mental pat on the back. He gestured to her glass. "Water?" he teased. Once he'd coaxed her into taking a tiny taste of his beer, but she had declared it was too terrible to drink. *Ah, there was only so much you could teach a good little religious girl from the farm.*

He swirled the amber contents of his drink and felt his temper rising. He took a long, slow swallow, watching her over the rim of his glass. She was the key; she would get him what he wanted. But he was tired of waiting. He put his glass down on the table with a thud and gave her a stern look. "So, is she there?" he demanded.

She gave her blonde curls a nonchalant toss and looked up with innocent eyes. "Who?" she asked petulantly.

He reached into the pocket of his jacket and slapped a photograph onto the plastic tablecloth. He didn't need to look at it; the soft brown eyes and sable hair were burned into his memory. "You know who," he said, his fury sharp and dangerous in the pit of his stomach.

She bit her lower lip, and her chin trembled. "But I thought you loved me," she whined. "Why do you want to find *her*?" Her gaze was riveted on the photo.

Working to control his impatience, he stared at the soft planes of the woman's face, pale-pink sculpted lips, eyes like dark pools. Something hard tensed inside him. After several seconds, he looked across at the girl wiping sulky tears from her large gray eyes. "Because," he began through clenched teeth, "she has something I want, and you, my good little church girl, are going to help me get it."

1

Mary Ann Berne stirred the third spoonful of sugar into her coffee and beamed. "A quilt auction and Valentine's Day party sponsored by Sew Welcome and the Olde Mansion Inn. It's a great idea. I love it, and Valentine's Day isn't far away now."

"It will be just the ticket for the winter doldrums," Sadie put in, her sharp blue eyes shining. "As co-owner of the Sew Welcome Shop and charter member of the Material Girls, I, Sadie Schwarzentruber, do heartily declare it will be a grand success."

Liz Eckardt smiled, warmed by the enthusiasm of her friends and fellow members of their quilting group. Sadie and Mary Ann had welcomed her with open arms and helped her navigate the unfamiliar waters of innkeeping.

She hadn't known what to expect when she gave up her successful Boston law practice and bought the inn in the heart of Amish country. But she had swiftly settled into Pleasant Creek, Indiana, and she thoroughly enjoyed providing a homey atmosphere and interesting adventures for guests of the inn. Several had returned for another visit.

Liz had balked when she first learned that she would be sharing space with the Sew Welcome Shop. The shop took up two rooms on the ground floor of the Olde Mansion Inn—an airy workroom and a fabric outlet that contained a wide variety of quilting goods. She had quickly realized that it was a "marriage made in heaven." So many of her guests were intrigued by quilting—a mainstay of Amish life.

Finding her Amish relatives, who had accepted her and become her friends, was the biggest miracle of all. It was quite an accomplishment for an "Englisher," as the Amish called anyone who was outside the order.

Yes, it had been an exciting transition, and even today there were new guests arriving. She hoped Sarah Borkholder and Kiera Williams, her two part-time employees, had finished all the preparations, including setting out the supplies for coffee and hot chocolate in the front sitting room. Pleasant Creek could be a winter wonderland but not without the help of a good fire and something warm to drink.

"I've tentatively secured the Order of the Otter Lodge for the event," Liz said. "It will be open to everyone in the community. The quilt auction will be the main attraction, but the hall is big enough to have a dance, with refreshment tables around the perimeter. The children's wing of the hospital really needs the funds for new equipment and furnishings. Judging by the quilts donated so far, along with the ones we're working on, we should be able to present a nice fat check to the administrator."

The quilt auction had been Naomi Mason's idea. And, as owner of the bakery Sweet Everything, she had promised to supply fancy cookies—her specialty. Liz glanced at the third member of the Material Girls present and realized that Naomi had been uncharacteristically quiet. "Don't you think so, Naomi?"

"Hmm?" she queried, looking around like a sleepwalker coming to.

"Earth to Naomi," Sadie said, clearing her throat and looking over the top of her magnifiers. Sadie never minced words, but her heart was as sweet as her tongue was sharp.

"Oh, I'm sorry," Naomi said apologetically. "I guess I was thinking of something else." She looked at Liz helplessly. "The auction—yes, it will be a real drawing card." She shook her dark shoulder-length hair and reached for her cup of coffee, which Liz saw was as full as it had been when they first sat down for a planning session.

A fairly recent transplant to Pleasant Creek, Naomi was to all appearances making a go of her business. Liz loved sitting in the cheerful-but-understated bakery with its white tables and chairs set against the backdrop of soft gray walls. Naomi knew how to achieve just the right touches with coral print paper place mats and carnations in bud vases. It wasn't so much the ambience of the bakery but the quality of her baked goods that kept customers returning again and again.

Looking at Naomi's slender face and willowy body, it was hard to believe her confession that at one time she had weighed close to two hundred pounds. Being surrounded by cupcakes and chocolate chip cookies all day without being tempted to eat them had to be a major challenge. But Naomi was very intentional about nutrition and keeping fit. She had conquered her weight problem in grand style.

At the moment, though, Naomi was nibbling her second cookie with frequent, nervous bites. Something was definitely bothering her. "Are you all right?" Liz asked in a hushed voice.

The others were out of earshot, Sadie having stepped into the shop area to check supplies, and Mary Ann having gone to wait on a customer. Liz and Naomi were alone in the large workroom.

She touched Naomi lightly on the shoulder. "Something's bothering you," she said softly. "Is it your mother?"

"No, she's okay. She's . . . the same." Naomi looked away. "It's my day to visit her though." She frowned as though depressed by the prospect.

Naomi's mother was a resident in a senior facility not far from Pleasant Creek. The Serenity Arms was a fine home with an excellent reputation. Liz knew that Naomi visited her mom regularly but seldom talked about her. In truth, Naomi hadn't shared a lot about herself at all since coming to Pleasant Creek. In spite of that, Liz had warmed to her immediately and now counted her as a friend—perhaps her closest friend.

"It must cost an arm and a leg to keep her mother in that place," Sadie had mentioned once. Sadie also knew "for a fact" that Naomi had paid cash for Sweet Everything. Having lived all of her seventy-plus years in Pleasant Creek, Sadie knew a lot about everybody, though to her credit she didn't gossip "unless it was absolutely necessary."

Naomi looked so dejected that Liz was stymied and a little bewildered. What was so depressing about visiting one's mother? *What I wouldn't give for a moment with my mom.* Not a day passed that Liz didn't think of Abigail Byler Eckardt, who for years had kept her past life a secret. Finding her mother's diary after her death had been the catalyst for Liz's coming to Pleasant Creek. She couldn't have imagined finding her mother's sister and brother—her aunt Ruth and her uncle Amos—plus a host of cousins in this wonderful Amish community, but that's exactly what had happened.

Liz regarded Naomi's averted gaze and concerned expression. Her chocolate-brown eyes clouded over like a gathering storm as she reached for another cookie and began nibbling nervously. This was completely unlike the Naomi she knew. What in the world was going on?

"I could go with you to see your mom," Liz suggested. Sometimes when visiting a family member—especially if the relationship or circumstances were difficult—it helped to take someone along who was completely objective.

"Oh, I couldn't ask you—"

"You didn't," Liz said quickly. "Everything is ready at the inn. The new guests won't arrive until after supper, and Sarah and Kiera will serve afternoon tea." She smiled into the troubled eyes of her friend. "I would enjoy keeping you company. Besides, I've never met your mother and I'd like to—if you think it's all right."

Naomi frowned, considering. She cocked her head and some of the gloom dissipated from her features. "I'd like that," she said softly. "And I promise we won't stay too long."

Fresh snow blanketed the fields and glistened in the brittle sunshine as they drove to the Serenity Arms Residence in Naomi's late-model Hyundai. Liz reveled in the Indiana landscape that in summer gleamed with glorious green radiance. Even now, in the grip of winter, it touched her with wonder.

The sky seemed like a designer quilt in a hundred shades of white—lavender-white, blue-white, gray-white. Like busy crafters, snowflakes sewed a border on a hemlock-covered hill, embroidered a valley, and stitched a ruffle on a porch rail.

"Just to warn you," Naomi said before opening the door to her mother's residence, "my mother may bore you with tales of my brother's heroics on the battlefield. It's all she talks about, and I'm afraid it can become rather tiresome."

"I didn't know you had a brother."

"Half-brother, actually, and I really didn't know him very well. Mother married my father after her first husband passed away. Willie John was sixteen when I was born." She pushed through the partially opened door with its bronze plaque signifying that "Moriah Mason" resided there.

Liz followed Naomi into a spacious private room where a woman well into her eighties sat in a plush lounge chair, her perfectly coiffed hair white as the snow outside. She wore a blue pantsuit accessorized with an attractive paisley scarf and gold jewelry. She stared pensively at her guests through pale blue eyes.

"Mother, this is Liz Eckardt." Naomi bent to kiss her mother's cheek. "Liz owns the Olde Mansion Inn and is one of the quilters in our group. You remember, I told you about her."

Mrs. Mason sat up straighter in her chair. Her lips moved in a polite hello, her eyes darting left and right. Perhaps she'd only recently awakened and was a little disoriented by a new face.

Liz stepped closer but refrained from stretching out a hand to take the delicate, blue-veined one that gripped the arm of her chair. "I'm so pleased to meet you, Mrs. Mason. Your daughter and I are good friends."

Mrs. Mason nodded. "Thank you," she said, and looked from Naomi to Liz and back again, blinking before turning abruptly to a photograph on a small round table at her right.

A young man in military uniform looked out of a gilded frame. Impassive, neither proud nor smiling. Dark brown hair, clean-shaven, studio perfect.

"My son is a hero," Moriah Mason said, eyes fastened on the photograph. A smile touched her thin lips. She was focused now—no more a dreamy-voiced octogenarian. "Did you know that every year on Memorial Day a wreath is placed on his grave? Every year he is remembered. The whole town turns out to honor him." Her eyes glittered with unshed tears. "My boy. My brave boy," she whispered.

Liz nodded, unsure how to understand Mrs. Mason's words. Did these memorials happen in real time or only in the woman's mind? Naomi hadn't said. Liz swallowed and smiled at the older woman. "You must be very proud of him."

She glanced at Naomi, who watched her mother indulgently—as one might a cherished child. But Mrs. Mason had yet to even acknowledge her daughter's presence. Liz turned to Moriah Mason. "You can be very proud of Naomi too," she said. "Her bakery is one of the most popular places in Pleasant Creek. Sweet Everything is making a healthy profit, Naomi tells me."

If the elderly lady heard her praise of Naomi, Liz couldn't tell. Her eyes remained fixed on the photograph. A silence ensued and presently the old woman looked up, her face a study in anxiety. She looked from Naomi to Liz and back again. "They will remember, won't they? There will be a wreath this year?"

"Of course, Mother," Naomi soothed. She maneuvered herself to obscure the photo and began to tidy up the area around her mother's chair. "I'll get you some fresh water—or perhaps you'd like some ginger ale?"

Mrs. Mason blinked, as though returning to the real world. She shook her head. "Nothing, dear, I'm fine."

Mentally, Liz pounced on the word *dear*, wanting to underscore it for Naomi, though there was little warmth in the utterance. *Oh, my friend*, she thought, *have you lost your mother before her time? I had no idea of your heartache.*

Liz kept up a running commentary—how lovely Mrs. Mason's flowers were, how beautiful her room—while Naomi gathered up soiled laundry and arranged scattered papers. Although the well-paid staff of Serenity Arms would certainly perform these duties for their residents, Naomi seemed compelled to care for her mother—the mother who lauded a son long gone and was oblivious to her living child's aching heart.

The uncomfortable visit ended quickly, as Naomi had promised. They headed back toward the inn—as quiet and subdued as the sieve of sky from which no more flakes tumbled. Liz hoped Stefan Meyer, the handyman she had recently hired for the season, was clearing the parking lot and walkways for the inn's guests.

"I'm sorry," Naomi mumbled, gripping the steering wheel with both hands. "Ever since Desert Storm, my mother hasn't been herself."

"No need to apologize," Liz said, puzzled. If Mrs. Mason had been this way for over twenty-five years—ever since her son died—it was nothing new for Naomi. Why was she acting so strangely? She was usually cheerful, joking with patrons of the bakery, eager to help in community projects and to join in on fun with the Material Girls. But at Sew Welcome today she had sat solemn and distracted, eating one cookie after another without seeming to taste them.

Did one get used to being ignored and feeling unloved while a sibling—even a half-sibling—was so overtly cherished? Liz wanted to apologize for Moriah's omission, to make it up to Naomi somehow. Maybe her mother's attitude was finally getting to Naomi.

"Naomi! Watch out!"

Naomi hit the brakes as an Amish buggy crossed the road from the left. The car skidded and whipped around the carriage like a spinning top. The startled horse reared, snorting and pawing the air.

"Whoa! Halt! *Bitte!*" the driver yelled as she struggled for control. The person riding in the buggy screamed.

Seconds that seemed like minutes passed with no impact. Silence. Both drivers had averted catastrophe. Liz felt her heart hammering. Naomi's face had drained of color.

"Hey, what's the matter with you, driving like that?" A young woman in a red coat and white fur hat leaped from the buggy, managing not to trip in her high-heeled boots. "You nearly killed *Mutter!*"

Liz stared at the unexpected apparition—the blonde hair flying loose under the fluffy hat, wide mascaraed eyes, hands in red-and-green striped mittens flapping in protest.

"Hush, Rachel!" said the driver, an Amish woman in black cape and bonnet. She held tightly to the reins as Naomi and Liz hurried to the buggy.

"I'm so sorry!" Naomi said. "I . . . I didn't see you coming. I—"

"Are you all right?" Liz called, shaking with relief. The woman seemed to be in control.

"We are fine, thank *Gött*." The graying woman had a round, pleasant face and solemn eyes. "And you—you are all right too?"

"Yes, yes!" Naomi sputtered. "I'm so sorry—"

"Don't you know there's a lot of these buggies around here?" accused the young woman, her wide-set gray eyes stormy.

"Rachel, get back in the buggy. Everything is fine." When the younger woman resumed her seat, the older woman nodded to Liz and Naomi. "All is well," she said. "We thank Gött." She lifted her chin and turned slightly in the seat. "I am Orpah Hausen, and this is Rachel—my daughter. She is visiting us from out of town."

Orpah Hausen. Liz knew the name and realized she'd seen Orpah around town, but this was the first time they'd actually met.

"Yeah, and even I know you gotta slow down around here!" came the pouting reproof from behind Orpah.

"Rachel! Please . . ." Orpah said.

Rachel gave an exasperated sigh and folded her arms over her crimson coat.

Liz figured that the girl was twenty-something and definitely not practicing Amish. She must still be "running around" as the Amish termed *"Rumschpringe." She's come to visit her family, Liz thought. She doesn't seem likely to repent and put herself under the authority of the church.*

Liz introduced herself and Naomi, who was still visibly shaken. After more mumbled apologies and assurances, they got back in Naomi's Hyundai and watched the buggy lumber off down the road.

Naomi spoke after several moments riding in tense silence. "It'll probably be a cold day in June when you go visiting with me again."

"Certainly wasn't dull," Liz said, trying to tease a smile from her friend's lips. "It was funny to see that fancy blonde jump out of an Amish buggy, wasn't it?"

But Naomi looked down, showing no trace of her usual good humor. She gripped the steering wheel tightly and squinted in concentration.

Liz sighed. It would be a blessing to get back to the Olde Mansion Inn, whip up a batch of poppy seed muffins, and sit around the fire in the comfortable parlor and get to know her new guests. She settled back in the seat with a prayer of thanksgiving for safety and the promise of a quiet evening.

2

When Naomi stopped to let her off at the Olde Mansion Inn, Liz felt a surge of relief. She loved coming home to her sturdy haven with its brick-red siding and fresh white trim. Snow had begun to fall again after its brief respite and was quickly blanketing the ground. The landscape was a wonderland. Even in winter, the backyard gazebo overlooking Jaynes Lake bore a nobility that beckoned visitors to its sheltering arms.

She watched as Naomi drove off without a backward glance. First, the meeting with Moriah Mason, who seemed to look through her daughter without seeing her, and then nearly crashing into an Amish buggy had left both of them reeling. Liz was definitely ready for that toasty fire and a strong cup of tea.

Stefan had shoveled the walk with his usual careful precision, though it wouldn't be long before he'd have to do it again. The winter wreath of woven branches and red berries that hung on the front door and the colorful mat at the entrance made a cheery sight. Everything about the inn was welcoming, and she looked forward to extending that warmth to the guests who awaited her.

Liz shut the door quickly against the cold and hung her coat in the hall before making her way into the sitting room. Kiera, wiry arms sheathed in a tatty green sweater, was pouring tea into cups for Violet and Vera Holmes, twins whom Liz remembered from their first visit to the inn. The Sew Welcome Shop was for them the charm of the Olde Mansion Inn. The sisters had spent a lot of time there during their first visit and might never have considered a winter vacation were it not for the allure of quilting right in the midst of Amish country. Interesting if quirky guests, the sisters brought an old-world charm to the inn. Liz was delighted that they had returned.

She rushed toward them. "Miss Holmes and . . . Miss Holmes!" she said awkwardly, extending her hand. Calling them Violet and Vera would be much easier, but their generation was strong on polite introduction. Besides, for the life of her, she couldn't remember which was which. "I'm sorry I wasn't here when you first arrived. I hope everything is satisfactory—" Liz stopped, suddenly realizing that the two were huddled together on the small sofa nearest the fire, one wearing a furry jacket and the other with an afghan wrapped around her shoulders.

"Everything is not satisfactory," huffed the one in the furry jacket. "Haven't you been paying your heating bill, Miss Eckardt?"

Vera. Silver hair coiled tightly around a narrow face, snappish brown eyes that Liz recalled had sparked with good humor before. The lady clearly found no humor in the current situation.

"Our room is cold as a barn!" Vera continued.

A softer voice chimed in. "Really, dear, it's quite chilly in that beautiful room we'd remembered so fondly." Violet glanced in shy disapproval at her twin and folded her hands in the lap of her lavender dress, a romantic blend of old lace and shiny shantung.

Liz looked from one to the other in confusion. On prior visits, both had been delightful guests, finding everything in Pleasant Creek to their liking and praising the features of the inn. They had requested the Rose of Sharon Room where they had stayed before. They had raved about the flowery quilt and white vintage furniture, and the delicate prints by early twentieth-century Indiana author and naturalist Gene Stratton-Porter.

She looked around for Kiera, realizing at the same moment that the sitting room did feel a bit chilly. Even Beans, her pet bulldog, was lolling in an undignified sprawl close to the fire.

"Something must be wrong with the furnace," Kiera said, sidling up close to Liz, her voice a stage whisper. "Sarah said it was cold upstairs while she was dusting the rooms."

"Where's Stefan?" Liz asked.

Kiera rolled her green eyes and adjusted the scarf over her hair. "He finished the shoveling here and went home to take care of things at his place."

"Call him. Tell him we need him." Liz felt the beginnings of panic. She didn't need this with new guests arriving.

"I did," Kiera said, giving her head a shake, "but no one answers. I suppose it's because he's outside. And you know he has a habit of forgetting his cell phone."

Liz forced herself to remain calm. "Well, keep trying." Turning back to Vera and Violet, she added in a cheery voice, "I'm sure it will be set to rights very quickly. In the meantime, stay here by the fire and have some more of these excellent scones."

Violet reached eagerly for the plate of pastries. Vera mumbled something under her breath that Liz tried not to hear as she punched in the furnace contractor's number on her cell phone. Only a few weeks ago he had done a complete check and declared the inn's heating system in perfect order.

While she waited for someone to answer, she nudged Beans, whose body was blocking some of the heat from the fireplace. She gave him a stern reprimand. He raised his head briefly and opened glazed eyes before dropping his big head back on the carpet. Though she'd been less than pleased to learn—only after she'd purchased the inn—that the lazy bulldog came with the place, she'd become very fond of him. But right now he definitely was not making himself useful.

Liz stepped into the adjacent foyer, out of earshot of her guests, when the receptionist picked up. "He's out on call?" she repeated, hearing her voice rise in pitch. "Liz Eckardt at the Olde Mansion Inn," she said and explained the situation as calmly as she could. "Please send him out as quickly as possible. I have three guests and more arriving; we must have the heating system up and running."

She slipped her phone back into her pocket and, wearing what she hoped was a confident smile, prepared to rejoin the ladies in the sitting room. She and the Material Girls had put their all into preparing for this special Valentine's Day week. With Sarah's and Kiera's help, Liz had scrubbed and cleaned until the inn sparkled. The menu was set, the kitchen exuding delicious smells to tempt the shyest palate. Everything was ready, but cold accommodations could ruin their plans.

In the confusion, she hadn't thought to ask who else had arrived. The advertising executive from Chicago wasn't due until evening. Another gentleman—a cousin of the Holmes sisters—was expected. She had booked him into the Sunrise Room, a single-occupancy accommodation with a blend of contemporary and antique furnishings, including a substantial desk. Its walls were white with brightly colored wall art and cushions. She'd instructed Sarah to tone down feminine accessories and Kiera to place a green ivy plant rather than the usual flowers in his room.

Fresh flowers were a signature amenity of the inn. They were easily obtained from the inn's lush gardens in warm weather but in winter had to be ordered at considerable expense. She hoped the ladies had found the flowers chosen for their room to their liking, something to take their minds off the temporary lack of heat.

As she reentered the sitting room, she was surprised to hear a high-pitched trilling sound. A small, square man with wire-rimmed glasses and tawny hair combed over his forehead tilted his head comically and repeated what sounded like "Sirrr, sirrr, sirrr." He wore a khaki photographer's vest over a charcoal flannel shirt and tan trousers. His feet, which were encased in hiking boots, made swift sidestep motions as though, like a hunter on safari, he couldn't wait to explore the jungle. Large eyes glittered behind his spectacles, or maybe it was the gold rims that added the incandescent sparkle.

Binoculars bobbing on his chest, he gestured avidly to Vera and Violet with small pink hands. "The Bohemian waxwing's song is quite distinctive. Mind you, it doesn't waver as much, and it's lower in pitch than the cedar waxwing's. Longer too than the Japanese waxwing's." He turned at Liz's approach. "Oh hello," he said brightly, smiling and extending a hand. "Felix Horner."

"Our cousin," Violet put in, blushing slightly as she often did around men. "We were just getting reacquainted."

Liz took his hand, which was surprisingly strong and warm. "Mr. Horner, I'm so pleased you have come. Tell me, is your room—" She broke off, hoping his warm hands meant his room wasn't freezing.

"Cold as a ptarmigan's wing, I'm afraid," Felix said without losing his pleasant smile. "But I expect the problem will be solved soon."

Liz was relieved that Felix Horner was taking the lack of heat with grace. Mental fingers crossed, she addressed the three guests. "We *are* working on the heating problem, and I'm sure all your rooms will be warm and cozy soon."

"I'm used to all kinds of weather," Felix said. "When you're on the hunt for a particular species, you find you can endure even the most inclement conditions." He tapped the binoculars perched on his chest. "I'm a birder, Miss Eckardt."

"I see," Liz said, though she didn't really. It was the first time a bird-watcher had checked into the Olde Mansion Inn. Maybe she should have assigned him the room with the Stratton-Porter prints of birds, but that would have risked the ire of Vera. "It must be difficult to find birds in winter in this part of Indiana."

"Oh my, no," he said, shaking his head and causing his jowls to wobble. "Winter is a great time for finding our feathered friends. And, mind you, a particular species of waxwing has been spotted in this part of Indiana. I've been on the lookout for a Bohemian for some time." His smile faded, and the dimple in his chin disappeared as he looked down at Beans, whose snoring was impossible to ignore. "He doesn't chase birds, does he?"

Liz smiled down at the dog, who lifted his head briefly as though affronted and then dropped it back onto his paws. She turned back to Felix. "You don't know Beans."

"I beg your pardon." Felix pushed out his chest, pigeon-like.

Liz gasped, realizing he had misunderstood. "No, I didn't mean it that way. Beans is the dog's name, and I can assure you that he doesn't chase anything."

"Oh. Well, I'm relieved to hear that." He put a hand over his binoculars, as though shielding them from deadly harm.

Violet smoothed a silver curl behind her ear. "Felix, I'm glad you came. Why, I don't think Sister and I have seen you since we were—what? Fourteen or fifteen?"

Liz tried to imagine the twins as teenagers. Vera had no doubt been the more serious of the two and kept her fun-loving sister from too much foolishness. Both had become teachers and lived comfortably. Now, having saved their money, they were enjoying their retirement. *Felix Horner as a teenager must have been something of a misfit or eccentric*, Liz thought as she took his measure. *If he wasn't then, he's certainly grown into it.*

"Likely, very likely," Felix said, responding to his elderly relative's remark. "You were budding young ladies, and I was but a toddler. A lot of swallows have flown over the barn since then, but here we are together." He smiled again, showing short, even teeth. "And may I invite you to accompany me in the morning, ladies? Mind you, it will be early. That's when conditions are optimal to locate the Bohemian—and other feathered friends, of course." He regarded his cousins hopefully. "I brought extra binoculars."

Violet looked undecided but mumbled something to show her pleasure at being asked.

Vera crossed her arms stolidly over her furry jacket and cleared her throat. "We might consider your offer, Cousin," she said with authority, then, with a meaningful glance at Liz, added, "if we're still here in the morning!"

Liz cringed. It was unmistakably a threat. Too bad Vera Holmes didn't possess some of Felix Horner's good-natured aplomb.

"Oh and you too, Miss Eckardt," Horner said in his high-pitched trill. "There's nothing like hearing the song of these delightful creatures in the early morn."

"That's very kind, Mr. Horner," she began.

"Do call me Felix."

"Um, yes. I mean, I appreciate the invitation to go bird-watching, but I'm sure I will be needed to attend to things here at the inn."

"Indeed!" harrumphed Vera, who clearly blamed Liz's lack of attendance to the heating system for her present discomfort.

Liz groaned inwardly. If she didn't hear from the contractor soon or find Stefan, the Holmes sisters might well pack up and leave. "Kiera, please bring some of those cinnamon scones—the warm ones that just came from the oven—and a pot of hot tea."

Liz's heart leaped when she heard someone at the door. *Stefan or the furnace repairman. At last!* She ran to answer it herself, though Sarah was already heading into the foyer.

The new arrival was clearly not Stefan or the hoped-for contractor. Instead, a tall, well-dressed man in his late thirties or early forties stood on the threshold, an expectant look on a face that could double for a Hollywood celebrity's. He wore an expensive-looking leather jacket over black chinos and a white silk scarf at his neck reminiscent of those worn by a World War I flying ace and carried a leather valise. "Shane O'Rourke," he said with an ingratiating smile. "I believe you have my reservation."

Momentarily stunned, Liz stammered something which to her own ears sounded completely inane. Mr. O'Rourke's looks as well as his name were impossibly romantic.

"This is the Olde Mansion Inn, isn't it?" he pressed, taking a step forward in black boots with shiny silver tips. White teeth flashed as he pronounced each word with careful diction.

"Yes, certainly," she managed. "And your room is ready. That is, it will be—"

His eyes narrowed in a moment of irritation, then quickly returned to their pleasant scrutiny.

"What I mean is, we seem to have a problem with our furnace. We've been trying to reach a repairman, but I'm afraid right now—well, the other guests are in the sitting room keeping warm by the fire. Perhaps you could wait there as well until the problem is solved?" She paused, half expecting an explosion or a cancellation.

"I see," O'Rourke said, passing a hand over his shiny black hair meditatively. "As it happens," he began slowly, "I have some experience with furnaces. I'd be glad to have a look. You never know, it could be something simple."

"Really?" Liz said.

"We should probably check the outside vent first. With all the snow that's been coming down, it might have gotten clogged. That could blow out the pilot light." He set aside the valise, zipped up his jacket higher and pulled on a pair of leather gloves.

Liz watched him grab the shovel by the door and head around the side of the inn. Moments later he returned, a look of triumph on his face. She led the way to the furnace in the basement and watched him relight it. Giddy with relief, she could have kissed him. Instead, she politely ushered him back upstairs and into the company of Felix Horner and the twins . . . and someone else.

Jackson Cross stood in the foyer carrying a small white-oak table—the one she had asked him to refinish for her. Besides being the mayor of Pleasant Creek, Jackson was a skilled craftsman and owner of the Cross Furniture Company that employed many of the Amish men in the area.

Sawdust mingled with melting snowflakes in his thick brown hair. He was handsome by anyone's standards in worn jeans, flannel shirt, and parka. *He must have come directly from his workshop without changing,* Liz thought. He set the table down and straightened to meet her gaze, hazel eyes alight.

"Jackson!" Liz said. She was always amazed at the way his presence could instantly lift her spirits. "You brought my table. Thank you so much." But he was staring beyond her to the tall stranger who had just become something of a hero judging by the effusive praise he was receiving.

"Um, Jackson Cross, this is Shane O'Rourke," she stammered. "He just relit the pilot light, and now we have heat in the inn again. Isn't that great?" In the seconds of silence that followed, she sensed a decided tension in the room.

For his part, O'Rourke seemed unruffled, his posture rigid as he passed into the sitting room.

The good-looking stranger had her a bit flustered. Did Jackson pick up on that? She felt a little swell of satisfaction. She and Jackson were just good friends. Still, she wouldn't mind if he was just a tad jealous.

3

"I must say, these breakfast turnovers are delicious." Vera's bad humor had obviously improved after a night's sleep in the cozy warmth of the Rose of Sharon Room. Thanks to Shane O'Rourke, the furnace had hummed along beautifully all night. Shortly after performing his deed of honor, he had retired to the second-floor room Liz had assigned him, and she hadn't seen him since. Perhaps he liked to sleep in; he certainly deserved it after performing his noble act.

Violet, dressed in a lilac wool pantsuit, turned to Liz with a blushing smile. "I must have another turnover. I know I shouldn't, but they are absolutely divine."

Liz smiled, remembering that previous guests had characterized Violet as the master of overstatement. It was one of her hallmarks, along with her penchant for all things purple. Kiera had remembered and placed a vibrant purple African violet in the Rose of Sharon Room. "Certainly," Liz said. She extended the cut-glass plate of pastries to Violet and Vera, the only guests at the table in the dining room. "So you decided against going bird-watching with your cousin?" she asked.

Vera sat back and folded her thin arms across her chest. She wore a Nordic sweater over a white blouse, corduroy slacks, and substantial-looking brogues. She pursed her lips into a frown. "I prefer to watch birds from a safe indoor location. Definitely not in the wee hours of the morning in the middle of winter." She gave her head a decided little snap.

"It must have been Felix I heard rummaging around overhead," Violet said pleasantly. "He's a sweet little man, don't you think? I hope he wasn't disappointed in us for not going bird-watching with him." She wrinkled her nose and gave a grand shrug of her shoulders. "Sister and I much prefer quilting to outdoor adventures—and we can hardly wait to peruse that marvelous fabric shop again." Bright blue eyes shone in her round face.

"The newest shipment Mary Ann ordered just came in yesterday," Liz said. "It should contain a wide variety of choices for you. We've also planned a tour of downtown Pleasant Creek, including some wonderful Amish shops." *The plows will have everything cleared soon*, she thought, venturing a glance out the window where flakes still swirled. Surely the snow would end soon, but in all the confusion last night she hadn't checked the weather report.

Before Vera and Violet left the dining room, Liz reminded them about the forthcoming quilt auction and Valentine's Day party. For today, Mary Ann and Sadie, co-owners of Sew Welcome, would keep the sisters busy and entertained. Sadie, in particular, would handle Vera's occasional snits of temper; the two had butted heads the last time the Holmeses had been in town, but before the week had ended they'd become friends. Actually, Vera had made certain that Sadie was still around before confirming her reservation.

"Anyone else down yet?" Sarah asked when Liz carried the Holmes sisters' dishes into the kitchen. Sarah had made herself indispensable at the inn. Now married, she clearly enjoyed working with Liz. The two had much in common, including the fact that Sarah's husband, Isaac Borkholder, had turned out to be Liz's second cousin.

"Nope," Liz said, placing the dishes on the counter. "Just the Holmes sisters." She grinned. "They're twins but they are so not alike. Vera's a bit like a drill sergeant, and Violet's a bashful flower." She gave Sarah's arm an affectionate pat. "But they're really fine ladies. I hope they enjoy their experience with us as much as they did last time."

"They weren't too happy yesterday," Sarah said softly, nodding her head of flaxen hair beneath the little black Kapp. "Thank Gött the furnace is fixed."

"Yes," Liz murmured, studying Sarah's gentle features. Reconnecting with her Amish roots had yielded surprising benefits for Liz. Their simple way of life and dependence on God and community were inspiring and brought a special dimension to the Olde Mansion Inn. *And to me*, she thought, as she looked into Sarah's eyes. "We are very fortunate that Mr. O'Rourke figured out what the trouble was." She pulled a storage tin from the shelf for the leftover pastries. "I haven't seen him yet this morning though. He's probably a late sleeper. That's what vacations are for, I guess."

"I'll make sure he has a hot breakfast when he comes down," Sarah said. "What about Mr. Horner?"

"I imagine he made good on his plans to go bird-watching," Liz replied. "I never thought of it as a winter activity, but he seems to think it's the perfect time of year." She couldn't help rolling her eyes when she thought of Violet's description of her cousin. *A sweet little man?* "Eccentric" came more to mind. "He certainly knows a lot about birds; I don't think he talks about anything else." And he likely knew every birdsong and had already treated them to several. *It could be an interesting week.*

Stefan was at work shoveling the walkways again this morning, his red tuque and muffler bright against the snowy backdrop. He'd driven up in his SUV and knocked at the door quite early, apologetic for not knowing about the furnace trouble the night before. "Confounded cell phone rattles my nerves," he'd said, "but I'm sorry you couldn't reach me."

Now he stood leaning on his shovel gazing out at the luminous countryside, rapt appreciation shining in his craggy face. She waved to him from the window and received a nod in response. Liz smiled. The man was a gentle, if proud, soul. Approaching seventy, he probably shouldn't be shoveling at all, but he balked at the tiniest suggestion of hiring someone to help him with the heavy work.

"Save some of those turnovers for Stefan," she said to Sarah as she let the curtain drop. She would urge him to come inside and rest, but he'd likely not stop until the last flake was history.

Stefan was retired from Cross Furniture Company. He still grieved the loss of his wife but seemed to find solace in helping out at the inn when Liz occasionally called him. There was something so lonely, so solitary about him. Who would watch over him in his golden years? Liz wished he could find someone to look after him, to keep him company on a cold winter night.

Liz helped Sarah tidy the sitting room and prepare the lemon bars that would be served later in the day. Then she donned her coat and boots. There was nothing she liked better than a walk in new-fallen snow—a chance to clear her head and enjoy Pleasant Creek's winter landscape. She had never imagined she would feel so connected to this place.

Liz called for Beans, who lay comatose by the fire. He'd been out earlier long enough to take care of business, but maybe he could be coaxed into an actual walk.

Or not. He simply stared at her and flopped back on the rug with a satisfied grunt.

She secured her jacket, pulled up her hood, and stepped out into the brisk air. The walkways were beautifully cleared; she must thank Stefan, who was probably putting shovels and salt away in the toolshed or working on something in the garage. She peeked inside both but saw no sign of him. She'd check in with him later and let him know how pleased she was with his work.

Liz reveled in the fresh air. A few snowflakes continued to swirl against a charcoal-gray sky and dampen her face as they drifted down. Walking two miles a day whenever she could helped her to keep fit, and she loved getting into the countryside beyond the inn. Jaynes Lake, opalescent and surrounded by evergreens, always drew her like a moth to a flame. She trudged toward it, enjoying the soft crunch of her boots on the frozen ground and feeling like an intruder in the deep silence. All of nature seemed hushed and sleeping. She felt like she might walk forever into some uncharted fairyland.

She recalled the season's first snowfall when she and Jackson had walked around the lake together. They hadn't talked very much, but she had been aware of a sense of warm well-being unlike anything she'd felt before. True friendship was a rare gift, but the hectic pace of her life as a corporate lawyer had argued against forming deep bonds. Thanks to her mother's gift of an Amish heritage, Liz was learning that meaningful friendships were more satisfying than any career.

Was she forming a bond with Jackson? Was she hoping for something even deeper than friendship? And what did the handsome mayor hope for?

She smiled, remembering him with sawdust and snow in his hair, how he had beamed proudly when presenting her with the finely finished oak table last night. Things had been in such confusion with the furnace trouble and her guests' displeasure that she hadn't even offered him a cup of coffee. All eyes had been on the charming Mr. O'Rourke. She had been lavish in her praise for the stranger's help and had hardly noticed when Jackson slipped out the front door. *I hope I thanked him properly*, she worried, but feared she had not.

Funny to be missing him now, to watch her single set of footprints and imagine him beside her, making a matching set. She liked the way the snowflakes felt on her face when no wind drove them, but now they were coming faster, thicker, quickly covering her tracks. Perhaps she hadn't been wise to walk so far from the inn.

Ahead and to her left stretched the Hausen farm, a patchwork of peaceful fields and gray-shingled buildings. Theirs was the closest farm to the inn, but the Hausens kept to themselves. It was the way of the Amish who generally didn't like mixing with Englishers. It saddened Liz, but she supposed she shouldn't expect to be welcomed by everyone simply because her mother had been Amish. She would always be an outsider in some people's eyes.

She studied the landscape. In summer, Orpah's husband—Ephraim, she thought his name was—would be working the fields or herding cows toward the barn, but now all activity was stilled and the land lay deserted. Or did it?

Something red attracted her attention. Just a quick flash and then it was gone. Someone running and quickly disappearing? But Amish women didn't wear red, and Amish men certainly didn't. Perhaps it was just a bit of cloth whipping in the wind.

Glancing across to the opposite side of the lake she realized that the panorama of trees and quiet fields had changed there as well. She detected movement near the forested area above the level of the lake. She hurried on and made out two men standing on the ridge above the water's edge. One looked oddly familiar in a dark parka and policeman's cap. Liz realized it was Chief Stan Houghton.

She secured her hood against the thickly falling snow and rushed around the lake. What were they doing there? A car on the adjacent road was heading toward the spot too—a car she recognized. Pleasant Creek PD. A chill raced up her spine.

She reached the road just as Officer Jack Gerst climbed out of his squad car, leaving the door standing open. She followed his loping gait and drew alongside him. "What's going on?" she asked breathlessly.

He didn't look at her or speak but sped toward Chief Houghton and Officer Dixon. Their cars were parked at the edge of the road with the passenger doors likewise ajar as though their drivers had been in a tremendous hurry. She stumbled along behind Officer Gerst, and when he stopped short, she nearly plowed into him. Then, after a dry branch suddenly snapped and fell away, all the world grew still.

She looked at the figure lying facedown, bright crimson staining the snow around him.

It seemed an eternity before anyone moved. Then Chief Houghton and the other officers knelt down and gently turned over the man's body. She gasped at the sight of Shane O'Rourke, his handsome features contorted in surprise or fear. Snow clotted his dark eyebrows and clung to the expensive leather jacket.

"No!" she breathed, her voice a squeaky whisper. She had a strange compulsion to gently sweep away the snow from his face and help him to his feet. But even before the officers leaned down to listen to his chest and press trembling fingers to his carotid artery, she knew he was dead.

An odd clicking noise penetrated the stillness, and Liz realized someone else was there. She glanced up to see Felix Horner, binoculars bobbing on his chest, standing to one side and shaking his head. He made soft tsk-tsking sounds like a dismayed old woman.

"I was tracking a great horned owl when I nearly stumbled over him," he said, quivery voice rising in shock or alarm. "I called 911 soon as I saw him. Is he—?"

"He's dead," Houghton said, looking up at the little man. Then he turned to Liz, acknowledging her presence for the first time. "Horner here says our victim is a guest at your inn. Is that right?"

She tried to speak but her lips felt frozen, and she couldn't tear her eyes away from the inert figure. She nodded miserably. "Could it be—suicide?" The terrible word cut through her as she spoke. O'Rourke was young, handsome, smart, and apparently successful. If he had taken his own life . . . What an unspeakable waste!

"Nope," Houghton said, rising but continuing to stare down at O'Rourke. "Bullet went through the right shoulder into the heart. No way this was suicide."

Shane O'Rourke has been murdered? Liz swallowed hard. One Olde Mansion Inn guest was dead, and another had found his body. It was all too terrible to contemplate. She was aware of the other officers moving about, cordoning off the area with ugly yellow tape, and of the medical examiner's long silver vehicle drawing up.

Officer Dixon talked quietly with Felix Horner who presented his identification and displayed the contents of his pockets. "No," she heard him say, "I never met him before last night when we both checked in to the Olde Mansion." The merry quality of his voice fell on her ear as wildly inappropriate for the dark situation in which they found themselves.

"I was so entranced by the call of the great horned owl, mind you," he continued. "It makes a low solemn sound, sort of like *ho-ho-hoo-hoo* or sometimes *whoo-hoo-whoo*." Incredulously, Liz listened as he imitated the bird's call for the officer, comparing it to the slightly higher-pitched female bird's voice.

Chief Houghton raised his eyebrows but kept his eyes on Liz. "I'll have to question Mr. Horner further," he told her in a low voice as he rifled through the dead man's pockets. "The other guests too." He gave her an indulgent smile. "Did you walk clear over here?"

She nodded, suddenly realizing that she was cold to the bone.

"I'll drive you back to the inn," he said. "Sorry about all this."

She had a history with Houghton. Stan Houghton, fiftyish and graying, was well respected in the community and known both for his shrewd peacekeeping and his ability to get along with the Amish, who preferred to avoid the police when possible. Pleasant Creek was a quiet community of hardworking people. Crime did exist here—and Liz had been involved in more than one instance when her perceptive abilities and clear thinking had earned the chief's admiration.

It was never good advertising for the police to show up at one's place of business. The Holmes sisters would be horrified to learn that their cousin had been the one to find the body. She wished she could shield the young and impressionable Kiera and softhearted Sarah from the grim news, but they would be all right. The Olde Mansion Inn had been touched by death before. The Material Girls gathered in Sew Welcome's workroom would be shocked, but they would quickly rally and set their minds to determining the particulars of the case.

"I understand," she said softly to the chief, who was extracting a small stash of dollar bills, a rumpled handkerchief, a package of spearmint gum, and . . .

The chief stopped suddenly and stared down at something in his hand.

Instinctively, Liz stepped closer to see what he was studying with such focused interest.

The chief was holding a dog-eared photograph of a young woman with soft brown eyes and hair the color of sable curling around her shoulders. Something was written on the bottom of the photo. *Your Mina.* Liz felt her heart beating like a wild thing trapped in a cage. There was no mistaking the lovely face of Naomi Mason.

4

When Liz, accompanied by Chief Houghton, drew up to the Olde Mansion Inn, they found the co-owners of Sew Welcome huddled in their coats on the front porch. Mary Ann stretched her elegant neck forward in tense expectation, and Sadie shaded her eyes against the brilliance of the snow. Before Houghton's car came to a complete stop, the inn's front door opened and a coatless Sarah stepped out, followed by an unusually animated Beans.

Liz let herself out of the chief's car and ascended the steps. "Talk about news traveling fast."

"Mary Ann saw the cars by the lake when she was coming in to work," Sadie said by way of explanation, but her sharp blue eyes were ablaze with curiosity. That she didn't immediately verbalize her questions in her usual brusque manner was likely due to the shock of seeing the police drive straight up to the inn on a quiet morning in February. Sadie pushed her way forward and caught Liz's arm. "Are you all right?"

Liz glanced at the anxious faces clustered on the porch. *Who else is watching behind windows? How soon before everyone is talking?* "I'm fine, but . . . let's all go inside. There's been an—incident." She pressed through the little crowd of concerned friends, Officer Stan Houghton following.

Back at the scene, Officer Dixon had ushered a slightly pale Felix Horner to his patrol car. The birder would have to give a statement at the police department and would no doubt be thoroughly interrogated there. The chief would probably question everyone else who was present at the inn last night and this morning. She had no doubt that he was particularly interested in Naomi. What was her picture doing in the dead man's possession?

Liz turned to Houghton but spoke loud enough for everyone to hear. "Perhaps we could all go into the sitting room. There's a fire going and Sarah will bring some hot coffee."

"Right away," Sarah said through chattering teeth.

Liz cleared her throat as the little group clustered in the sitting room fixed her with curious eyes. This news would come as a blow, a disturbing intrusion on her guests' plans for an idyllic getaway.

Vera and Violet sat forward in their chairs, hands folded over sewing projects that lay untended on their laps. Clearly, they had heard the news as well, though they hadn't gone out on the porch. *This may be particularly hard for them because of Felix*, she thought. She cleared her throat. "It's Mr. O'Rourke—the guest who arrived last night," she began. "He's been found near Jaynes Lake."

Gasps of surprise followed, then silence, giving her space to continue.

"Mr. Horner came upon him while he was out bird-watching. He called 911, but unfortunately . . ." She looked down at her hands that were sweaty and cold. "I'm sorry to tell you that Mr. O'Rourke is dead."

Vera was first to find her voice. "You mean that fancy man who fixed the furnace? Was he sick? Was it a heart attack?"

Houghton broke in. "I'm afraid Mr. O'Rourke was murdered. He was shot, apparently from the ridge above the lake, and his body was dragged up to the tree line."

The silence in the room was palpable as the stark imagery soaked in.

Then Violet asked in a trembling voice, "But who? Who would want to kill that nice man?"

The truth was, no one knew the nature—nice or not—of Shane

O'Rourke. He had billed himself as an advertising executive who wanted to vacation in this part of Indiana. Liz couldn't help wishing she had done a background check. Especially when the chief told her that O'Rourke's wallet contained no driver's license or photo identification and no credit cards. Here was someone who clearly did not want to be identified—unless someone had removed those items, leaving only a few dollars and Naomi's picture.

"And where is our cousin?" Violet continued, pushing out her lower lip as though his absence were a personal affront. She looked as though she might cry.

"Mr. Horner is giving us a statement at police headquarters," Houghton said. "It's just routine, since he's the one who found Mr. O'Rourke." Despite his tough exterior, the police chief could be surprisingly gentle. "He'll be released in due course," he added. "In the meantime, I'd like to hear from each of you about your knowledge of the victim and your whereabouts this morning."

"How long?" Liz asked. "I mean, how long do you think he has been there? Mr. O'Rourke, that is."

"We don't have the medical examiner's report yet. It's hard to pinpoint because a body in snow or ice is preserved to some extent. Takes longer for rigor mortis to set in." He stroked his chin with blunt fingers. "The weapon hasn't been located either, and with all this snow . . ." He stopped as though realizing he'd been thinking out loud. He cleared his throat. "We'll continue the search, but we think he was probably killed within the last two to three hours."

Sarah's face paled even further, and the cup rattled on the saucer as she handed Chief Houghton his coffee.

Tender Sarah, Liz thought. To her, murder was anathema, as it was to most people, Amish or English.

Chief Houghton took a sip of the coffee Sarah had given him

and then pulled out his smartphone, his apparent mode of choice for note taking. Liz found it amazing that he could navigate the device so rapidly with his thick fingers.

He turned to Liz. "Let's start with you. What were you doing in the area this morning?"

"I was taking a walk," she said. "Sarah and I began serving breakfast at seven. We cleaned up in the kitchen, and then about nine o'clock I started out."

"Where were your guests at the time?" Houghton asked, leaning back slightly in the straight-backed occasional chair.

"The ladies—that is, Vera and Violet Holmes—were the only guests in the dining room." She looked at them apologetically and continued. "Mr. Horner told us last night that he planned to go bird-watching early, so we didn't expect him. We didn't know what was keeping Mr. O'Rourke."

"Yes, we thought the dear man was sleeping late," Violet broke in. "He deserved his rest after saving us all from freezing to death." She stopped abruptly and frowned. "Oh dear," she finished.

"Our furnace went out," Liz explained, hastily covering Violet's unfortunate choice of words. "Mr. O'Rourke unclogged the outside vents and got the furnace working again. I showed him to his room, and that was the last time I saw him until—" Liz bit off the words and swallowed hard.

The chief nodded to an officer waiting by the front door, gesturing for him to search the room for O'Rourke's personal effects. "Any other guests registered at this time?" Houghton asked.

Liz shook her head.

Houghton took another sip of coffee and set his cup on the table by his chair. Looking across at the Holmes sisters, he asked kindly, "And where did you go after breakfast?"

Vera, true to form, didn't take Houghton's interrogation kindly. She leaned forward, her sharp eyes boring into the chief's. "We went to our room to brush our teeth, of course," she said with considerable venom.

"Yes, and we didn't come down until about half an hour ago," Violet put in. "We were waiting for the shop to open. We plan to do some serious quilting this week."

Sadie, who had been sitting close to Liz, spoke up. "Sew Welcome opens at ten o'clock, as you know, Chief. Mary Ann and I arrived only a few moments ago. That's when we saw your car and the commotion across the lake." She gave him a stern look. "Liz and the Olde Mansion Inn don't need this kind of publicity. I trust your department will find whoever is responsible and quickly!"

Liz couldn't help the smile that came to her lips as Sadie defended her honor.

Houghton met Sadie's penetrating gaze head-on; he could hold his own with prickly citizens. Still, his response was measured and polite. "You can be assured we will leave no stone unturned, but we'll need your cooperation."

Liz and the Material Girls had more than once helped the police solve crimes in Pleasant Creek. Whether the police asked for help or not.

Mary Ann, who had been listening with grave but perceptive eyes, spoke up, cutting off whatever Sadie was about to say. She gave her longtime friend a warning glance. "Of course, Chief. We are all shocked that this could happen in Pleasant Creek, especially to one of Liz's guests."

Violet nodded and looked at Vera, who sat stoically next to her, arms crossed over her Nordic sweater. Liz drew in her breath. *If the twins thought a cold welcome on their first night was the worst that could happen during their winter vacation, what are they thinking now?*

Chief Houghton rose and carried his coffee cup to the wheeled serving tray that Liz had bought at a recent auction. Apparently, he had learned all he needed for now from the group assembled there. He thanked them briefly and left the room. Liz followed him to the foyer where he pulled on the boots he had left by the door and zipped up his jacket. "Officer Bowles will gather Mr. O'Rourke's personal effects, and we'll need to see his car."

"He didn't register a car, Chief." Liz drew in her breath. *How did he get to Pleasant Creek from Chicago?* "I didn't see a taxi or anything. We were all so wrapped up in the trouble with the furnace . . ."

He pondered this for a few quiet seconds, then asked, "Is there anything you can tell us about Mr. O'Rourke?"

"He said that he was an ad executive from Chicago, but beyond that he was a stranger to all of us." She shook her head, wishing she could dispel the image of the man couched in bloodstained snow. "As far as I know he has no ties whatsoever to Pleasant Creek or to anyone here." But obviously he knew someone. Liz felt a lump form in her throat. She knew the chief would ask about Naomi. She tried to imagine how her friend would take the news of O'Rourke's death. What would Naomi say when she learned that her photograph was found on his body?

Houghton rubbed his lips thoughtfully, drew in a long breath, and released it.

"You're going to see Naomi, aren't you?" Liz said in a low voice. *Naomi is already upset about her mother*, she thought. *Now she's about to receive another blow.* At Houghton's affirmative nod, she said firmly, "I'd like to go with you. I think Naomi might need some moral support."

Houghton raised his eyebrows, considering. After a few seconds, he nodded. "May not be a bad idea. I'm heading over to the bakery now."

Sweet Everything was located next to the inn. Had Naomi seen the police car? Had she heard anything? She hadn't come running over to investigate, but then, if she was busy in the kitchen or serving guests, she may not have paid any attention to what was going on next door. "Let me grab my coat. Sarah and Kiera can handle things here for a little while."

———

The chief was quiet as they walked to the bakery. Liz knew he must be frustrated by the lack of clues gained at the scene of the crime—heavy snow, an iced-over lake, no witnesses, and no identification found on the body. How odd that O'Rourke carried no credit cards or other distinguishing information. What had happened to it? Surely his room would yield some clues. She recalled that he had been carrying a small valise when he'd arrived.

They walked quietly, heads bent against the snow. She could see that Houghton was taking in the neatly shoveled walks surrounded by the inn's idyllic landscape. "Was anyone else around besides Mr. Horner and the women inside?" he asked. "Anyone you saw on your walk maybe? Or working in the area?"

Quickly her mind went to the flash of red she had seen not far from the place where O'Rourke had been found. Just a quick glimpse. Someone running, but in an instant whoever or whatever it was had disappeared.

"Didn't I see Stefan Meyer working here earlier? He might have seen something."

Stefan? Liz's stomach lurched. She had waved to him from the window, and he had waved back. In his bright red ski cap and muffler. *But when I went out for my walk later, he was gone.*

Houghton paused at the entrance to the bakery, a quizzical look on his face. "Liz?"

She fiddled with the zipper tab on her coat, knowing Houghton was waiting for a response to his question. "Stefan was here early in the morning to clear the walks," she said. "But I didn't see him when I went out." She chewed her lip. Stefan hadn't come inside the kitchen for Sarah's scones either, which he loved. Where had he gone?

"I thought I saw something just beyond the Hausen farm," she began haltingly, "but it was only for a second. Just a flash of color . . ." *Stefan's muffler whipping in the breeze as he fled the scene?* But that was crazy. Stefan was the gentlest of men in spite of his gruff manner of speaking. *And he didn't even know Mr. O'Rourke. Did he?*

"A flash of color," Houghton repeated. He waited out Liz's silence.

"It might have been a person," she said. "Or maybe an animal or a flag flapping in the wind . . ." She pressed her lips together in thought. "It was snowing heavily and the wind was whipping up. I couldn't say what it was. Or who . . . if it was a who."

"Hmm." Houghton considered. "A flash of color. What color?"

"Red," Liz said quietly.

"Hmm."

She didn't elaborate. She would not mention Stefan's scarlet tuque and muffler. That he had anything to do with this awful business was just plain ludicrous. The thought was as crazy as the involvement of sweet, generous Naomi, who was about to be confronted with some awful news.

5

The bell over the door of Sweet Everything tinkled as the chief opened it and stood aside for Liz to enter. At mid-morning the shop was a hive of activity, its small white tables occupied with consumers of Naomi's special pastries and cups of fresh-brewed coffee. The fragrant warmth wrapped around Liz. She wished they had come to enjoy Sweet Everything's ambience, not to confront one of her best friends with questions about a murdered man.

Jenny Crenshaw, a part-time employee, was taking orders at the counter where customers picked up their purchases. A fiftyish woman with an angular face, penciled brows, and graying hair, Jenny was a recent widow. With two children away at college, she seemed to enjoy working and interacting with Pleasant Creek's citizens. Some said she was a bit free with her tongue. Now, her eyebrows rose with unspoken questions.

Customers reacted with heightened interest, casting anxious glances as Chief Houghton stepped up to the counter. A policeman, decked out in uniform and peacekeeping gear, always elicited notice, Liz supposed, but in the suddenly subdued atmosphere the chief's voice seemed unusually harsh. "We're here to see Miss Mason."

"She's in the kitchen," Jenny said without taking her eyes off the chief's badge. "I'll get her."

Liz touched the chief's elbow. "Naomi has a little office next to the kitchen. Why don't we just go on back. We can talk there."

Houghton nodded, extending a hand for her to lead the way.

Naomi was drawing a tray from the oven as they entered the

kitchen. She likely hadn't heard them because her back was to the door—or else because she was used to her helpers coming and going. In the brief seconds before she turned around, Liz took in the slender back bent over the rack, swift hands encased in flowered oven mitts, dark hair drawn into a smooth chignon.

A sense of dread washed over Liz. *What kind of trouble is Naomi in?*

"Liz?" Naomi's face, flushed with heat, seemed to grow suddenly pale. Her brown eyes widened as she glanced from Liz to Chief Houghton.

"Hi, Naomi." Liz stepped closer. "Sorry to bother you; I know you're busy . . ." She faltered, tried again. "Chief Houghton needs to talk to you, and I asked to come along. Someone's been . . ." She heard the nervous pitch of her own voice as she struggled to explain that a man had been found dead with her friend's picture in his pocket. *So much for trying to ease things for Naomi.* "Can we go into your office?"

Naomi slipped out of the butcher-style apron and laid it on the counter with the freshly baked pastries. Wordlessly, she moved into the alcove off the kitchen that held a desk and three chairs. The little office was characteristically neat and tidy with a single pink rose in a bud vase on the antique white desk. Though there was no door to close, the small space effectively closeted them from the hubbub of the bakery.

The chief spoke kindly but wasted no time. "Miss Mason, do you know a man by the name of Shane O'Rourke?"

Naomi looked from the chief to Liz in confusion, then gave a measured response. "No, I'm afraid I don't."

Houghton reached into the pocket of his jacket and laid the photograph on the desk's smooth surface. "Can you explain why your picture was found on his body, Miss Mason?"

Naomi peered down at the photo, the wrinkles in her forehead deepening. She looked up at Liz with frightened bewilderment.

"Shane O'Rourke was a guest at the inn," Liz began. "Just arrived last night. He was young—late thirties, early forties perhaps. Well-built and well-spoken." She drew her breath in sharply and let it out in a defeated rush. "One of our other guests discovered his body on the other side of Jaynes Lake. He was killed this morning."

Naomi gasped; she stared first at Liz, and then Chief Houghton. "That's terrible, but . . . but I don't know . . ."

The chief sat forward, hands folded in his lap. "I must ask you where you were earlier this morning—say between the hours of seven and nine."

"I was right here at the bakery, along with my assistant, Candice Woodhouse, since five a.m." Naomi looked indignant. "Why are you asking these questions?"

"Miss Mason, do you own a gun?"

Naomi nearly jumped out of her chair. "No! I've never owned a gun. I would never have one in my house! Why are you . . .?"

"Please, Miss Mason," Houghton said, speaking in a conciliatory tone. "At this point, we don't know what happened or who might have murdered Mr. O'Rourke."

"Murdered?" she repeated. "But I don't know anyone named O'Rourke."

"Your picture was found in his pocket," Houghton said with exaggerated patience. "At this moment you're the only lead we have. We need your help." Reclaiming the photo, he said simply, "I must ask that you don't leave town. We'll need to talk to you again."

When he was gone, Naomi dropped down onto the chair. Clearly she was upset. *As would anyone be in similar circumstances*, Liz thought. But there had to be a reason O'Rourke carried her photograph. Surely she knew that the police wouldn't stop until they connected the dots.

"Naomi, I'm so sorry about this. I know it's a terrible shock." Liz came around the desk to place a hand on her friend's shoulder.

Naomi clutched her arms at her elbows and closed her eyes, as though to shut out the world.

"It was signed 'Your Mina,'" Liz prodded softly. The chief hadn't mentioned that to Naomi. "Does that mean anything?"

She opened her eyes slowly and began to sway back and forth. After a moment she said with soft surprise, "Mina. He called me Mina."

"Who, Naomi?"

A long silence dragged on before Naomi asked, "Tell me, did this O'Rourke have eyes like black pools and a cleft in his chin? Did he speak with exaggerated enunciation as though everyone around him must be deaf or simple?"

Liz nodded hesitantly. Naomi's description of the man was accurate. *She knew him!* "What is it, Naomi? Who is he?"

Her voice seemed to come from some faraway place. "Trevor Winston. It was a very long time ago—nearly ten years. I was . . ." Her eyes fixed on something unseen. "I met him at a very vulnerable time in my life when I desperately needed someone. He was charming and attentive. But I didn't really know him until . . ." She broke off, lost in nostalgia.

Liz stared at her friend. "Do you mean to say that Shane O'Rourke is—was—really this Trevor Winston?"

"He called me 'Mina,'" she continued, as though Liz had not spoken. "He said 'Naomi' was prudish and old-fashioned, that I should have a classier, more modern name. And he'd make a joke of it. He said, 'I'll call you Mina because you're mine-a.'"

"Oh, Naomi," Liz breathed. The atmosphere in the little room grew heavy with silence.

As though the grim news had just sunk in, Naomi whispered, "Trevor is dead?"

"I'm sorry," Liz said gently. *Had she once loved him? Did she* still *love him?*

"There's nothing between us anymore," Naomi said. "I broke it off ten years ago. And I have no idea why he'd want to keep my picture." Her face darkened. "I wish I'd never given it to him. I never ever wanted to see him again." She shivered. "I'm sorry someone killed him, but it wasn't me."

"Of course it wasn't," Liz assured her.

"I didn't know you were talking about Trevor until you asked about the signature. No one else ever called me 'Mina,' so it had to be him. I suppose the chief will think I was lying to him."

"No, but you need to tell him that you knew this man. You need to tell him everything. And soon." No doubt she'd be called on to identify the body. The thought of Naomi having to look at that marble-like face and those cold, contorted lips was horrifying.

"It's just like Trevor to change his name; he was good at subterfuge. The last I heard he was headed for prison—he conned a lot of people out of their money. It's no wonder someone decided to pay him back."

The bitterness in her voice surprised Liz. Naomi was the kindest of souls, always willing to give someone the benefit of the doubt. This man must have really hurt her. She struggled to find the right words. "Don't worry. The police will investigate and find the truth."

"But everyone will think . . ." Her eyes darted around the room. "And who knows what my customers and staff might be thinking?" Naomi bit hard on her lip. "*You* believe me, don't you?"

"Of course I do. We all do," Liz responded quickly. The "we" she had in mind were the Material Girls who had seen each other through thick and thin with an intense loyalty. But there were others in Pleasant

Creek who would be whispering about Naomi, thinking the worst. *Can she really be involved? Is there more to this than she's saying?* She'd definitely been distracted lately, nearly causing an accident on the way back from the visit to the nursing home. *Or is she just overworked and stressed between her business and caring for her mother? And now she's the focus of a police investigation!*

"Look, this has been a terrible shock for you. Why don't you go home and rest?" Liz squeezed Naomi's shoulder. "Jenny can handle things here. And doesn't that young Lily Bauerman come in after school to help with the afternoon customers?"

Naomi brushed back the strands of hair that had strayed from her chignon and nodded. "I'll go home when the lunch crowd is gone." She hesitated. "And thanks, Liz, for not leaving me to face the police alone."

"I'm here for you, Naomi."

Liz left her bent over her desk, her head in her hands. When she stepped out of the bakery, the snow had stopped, abandoning its heavy white coat on the ground. She snugged her own coat tight around her shivering body and hurried back to the inn. She knew the police were still searching the area on the other side of the lake, and she didn't want to look in that direction. She didn't want to be reminded of man's dark intrusion into nature's lovely winter light.

She hesitated at the garage before going in the back door of the inn. Stefan was back. The thought then came unbidden: *Back from where?*

She stepped inside the garage and found Stefan standing over a sheet of plywood settled on twin sawhorses. An electric sander lay idle on the wooden surface. His large hands hung at his sides. He wasn't a big man but had a strong build and a thick shock of white hair. She noticed an uncharacteristic stoop to his shoulders that made him seem older, almost fragile. He appeared to be staring out the window in contemplation, but he turned when she said his name.

White eyebrows furrowed over slightly rheumy blue eyes. His complexion, usually ruddy from outdoor work, appeared pale in the dim confines of the heated garage. His expression changed suddenly, and Liz knew that he'd heard the news. Wherever he had been when she stepped out for a walk, he knew a man had died. "Miss Elizabeth?"

He refused to call her "Liz," in spite of her frequent invitations to do so. Secretly, the old-world chivalry touched her, and she liked him for it.

"Are you all right?" he asked quietly.

Suddenly weary, she leaned against the wall and nodded. "You?"

"The police were here," he said. "Nasty business." He shook his head slowly. "You never know who you're rubbing shoulders with."

"Had you ever seen him before?" she asked. Her eyes went unbidden to the red scarf hanging from an oversized nail over his navy peacoat.

A muscle worked in his jaw, and he narrowed his eyes at her. "That's what the police wanted to know."

Did it sound like she was accusing him? She hadn't meant to.

He shrugged. "He wanted to know where I was this morning too." The blue eyes looked through her. Stefan was proving to be a perceptive man.

"I know you were here very early shoveling the walks, and I wanted to thank you . . ." She paused before finishing her sentence. "But when I came outside to take a walk I couldn't find you."

Stefan placed a hand over the sander and patted it. "I realized I had left my sander at home and went to get it." His eyes drifted briefly to the floor. "The police wanted to know if I saw anyone, talked to anyone. I stopped home long enough to feed my dog and bring in some logs from the woodpile." He raised his chin, met her gaze. "Then I came back. That's all."

"They've been questioning everyone," she said apologetically. Her mind was working full tilt. Stefan only did a job for her here and there. He didn't have to punch a clock, and he always finished his work. But she didn't know what he did on his own time. Her thoughts repelled her. It was beyond belief that he had anything to do with O'Rourke—or Winston—or whoever the murdered man was.

"I'm sorry," he said after a few beats of silence. "Sure isn't a good way to start a week with your guests. Anything I can do, you just call." His lips formed a small, ironic smile as he patted the bulge of his cell phone in the pocket of his shirt. "I'm keeping her close now."

More penance for not being available when the furnace went out. She returned his smile, knowing he found modern technology, even his outdated flip phone, bothersome. She could recall the protests of Sadie, who likewise had little use for electronic devices. "Smartphones were made for dumb people. And they're getting dumber all the time!" Sadie had said.

She searched the rugged face she'd come to appreciate, the man Jackson had relied on at the furniture factory for so many years. Whoever the guilty party or parties were, and whatever the source of that flash of red, it couldn't possibly involve Stefan. Could it?

"Thanks," she said quietly and opened the door, letting in a rush of cold air. "I better get back to my guests." She grinned sardonically.

"There's one good thing, though. At least they can't take off for a more restful locale. The chief made it clear that no one leaves town until the investigation is over."

6

Liz took a bite of the caramel apple pie that Mary Ann had set by her place in Sew Welcome's spacious workroom. Everything Mary Ann Berne made was delicious, especially pie, but Liz found herself chewing without tasting.

The day had passed quickly as Liz saw to the needs of the inn's guests, and now an informal meeting of the Material Girls was in session. Plans for the Valentine's Day party and quilt auction had to be discussed. In spite of the events of the past two days, they had a commitment to the children's wing of the hospital.

Mary Ann was in charge of reservations; Sadie was responsible for gathering the donated quilts and seeing that they were transported to the venue. Liz and Naomi headed a committee to plan the party, complete with music, decorations, and food.

Naomi was staying close to the bakery, but Opal Ringenberg, Sadie, Mary Ann, and Liz were gathered around the wide craft table. Caitlyn Ross, the youngest member of their group, had been unable to make the meeting due to her shift at the hospital where she was an emergency-room nurse. As was often the case, the four friends were enjoying Mary Ann's signature refreshments. "Coffee and pie before business," she announced.

Opal's usually gentle voice took on an excited tone. "Here she is in the ballerina outfit I bought her." Opal always grew more animated when the topic of conversation was her newest granddaughter. "She is sweet, isn't she?" A photo of a chubby smiling toddler passed from hand to hand with everyone making suitable comments on the charming traits of Madison Ruby.

Mary Ann sat down across from Liz and fixed her with concerned brown eyes. "Eat," she coaxed softly. "After all that's been happening, you need nourishment."

"Thanks," Liz said, cutting into the pie with renewed vigor lest she offend Mary Ann. "It has been a very long day."

Mary Ann had made fresh coffee to accompany the pie, and the soothing aroma of the Irish crème brew filled the air.

"You all right?" Mary Ann asked, tucking a strand of her silver hair behind her ear. Although in her sixties, she looked much younger and possessed an excellent fashion sense—down to her elegantly finished fingernails, which today matched the color of her turquoise blouse.

"Of course she's not all right," Sadie snapped. "Who could be all right after discovering a dead man who turns out to be one of her own guests?" She gave Liz a mothering look and quickly resumed her take-charge attitude. "The chief gave all your guests and employees the third degree—us, too, for that matter—but I suppose he had to."

Liz favored her friends with a grateful smile. In spite of the large number of customers who had patronized the shop that day—likely curious about the goings-on at the inn—Mary Ann and Sadie had kept the twins busy all afternoon. Between quilting and enjoying generous servings of apple pie, Vera and Violet had something to think about besides the investigation.

"Thanks for helping out with the Holmes sisters," Liz said. "A thing like this could ruin their whole trip, but they seemed almost happy at coffee hour this afternoon—Felix Horner too." He had taken the mandatory questioning at headquarters quite well, she realized with some relief, and upon his return had entertained everyone with unusual facts about birds in winter. "He told us that swifts and hummingbirds can slow down their metabolism on cold nights. And the common poorwill actually goes into hibernation."

"Really!" Opal's prim mouth made an astonished *O*.

"Yes, according to Felix, it wedges itself into a rocky crevice somewhere and waits out the winter just like a bear. In spring it wakes up and goes back to hunting for food."

"The man's a walking Wikipedia when it comes to birds," Mary Ann marveled.

"Complete with sound effects," Liz added, rolling her eyes and reproducing in her mind his many warbles, whistles, and trills.

"So the funny little man is quite recovered after finding a fellow vacationer dead? Had they known each other?" Sadie wanted to know.

"He said he never laid eyes on him until he registered at the inn," Liz said. "And he's quick to point out that he has nothing to do with guns. The only thing he shoots with is his camera."

"Well, the police will check him out thoroughly. You can be sure of that," Sadie said with conviction. "The one who reports a crime is always the prime suspect. They'll watch him like a hawk—no pun intended."

"I certainly hope so," Mary Ann said. "They might even check out Vera and Violet too. Even sweet old ladies have been known to commit murder—though we women are usually a bit more inventive when it comes to methods."

Sadie gave Mary Ann a withering look from across the table. "Lumping us in with the baddies of the world, are you?"

The lightness of the exchange lifted some of the gloom Liz had been feeling, but the cloud that had descended over them all was not likely to dissipate any time soon. Someone had committed murder, and everyone had to be considered as a possible suspect. Liz thought it more likely that a person unknown to them—probably out of O'Rourke's past—had followed him to Pleasant Creek, exacted his revenge, and fled, taking the weapon with him. *Or her*, her mind amended.

"Is Naomi going to be all right?" Mary Ann asked, voicing the question on everyone's mind since Liz had told them of her visit to the bakery.

"The news came as a shock to her," Liz said, "especially when the chief told her that her photo was in the victim's pocket. But she hadn't seen O'Rourke—or should I say Winston?—for ten years. She broke off a relationship with him when she learned that he wasn't who he pretended to be."

Sadie had been aghast when Liz told her about the chief's visit to Naomi. "The very idea!" she fumed. "Besides, Naomi was in the bakery all morning. Surely the police are satisfied that she wasn't involved." She pushed out her lips in an expression of disapproval. "The chief should know better than to suspect our Naomi of something like that!"

Our Naomi. That's how the Material Girls perceived her. And they would defend her from any and all accusations. *As will I,* Liz thought. *But something has been bothering her. Could it have anything to do with this Trevor Winston?*

Eager to put her troubling thoughts aside, Liz asked Sadie for a report on the quilts available for auction. "Will we have enough, do you think?"

"We received two more donations today—one from Cora Hostettler, and it's a beauty! A Double Wedding Ring—probably the most popular quilt the Amish produce. Cora is one of the best quilters I've ever seen. That she happens to be my cousin is neither here nor there . . ." Sadie's lips turned up in a self-satisfied smile.

The truth was that Sadie's work ranked right up there with the best; the Material Girls and just about everyone in Pleasant Creek knew it.

"We have a Star of Bethlehem from Amy Fischer in the most gorgeous powder-blue and purple colors. I'd love to place a bid on it myself." Sadie's eyebrows rose sharply over her reading glasses. "And the Holmes sisters are helping us with a group project we've been working on forever, bless them. I thought we'd never finish that complicated Jacob's Ladder—or 'Gone to Chicago,' as Vera calls it."

"That quilt pattern has so many different names, I can't keep track of them," Mary Ann said. "I call it Stepping Stones, but whatever its name, it will be a popular offering."

Opal displayed a copy of the ad she had prepared for *The Pleasant Creek News & Views*, which had been running for ten days. With the auction fast approaching, they were soon to see how people would respond.

If only the investigation is cleared up in time so everyone can really enjoy the event, Liz thought. *Life goes on.* The timeworn cliché passed through her mind. Life might go on for some, but not for Trevor Winston.

As planned, they adjourned the informal meeting early. They'd all put in long hours on a difficult day. Though Liz always found the Material Girls' company comforting, she looked forward to some time to put up her feet and reflect on all that had transpired. She walked her friends to the door, waited while they donned their boots and coats, and urged them to drive safely. Though streets and roads had been plowed, the temperature had dropped significantly. There would be patches of ice to contend with.

She lingered, watching through the long window beside the door as their cars disappeared. She was about to turn the double lock when headlight beams swept around the foyer and stopped. Someone stepped out of a familiar pickup truck and hastened up the walk with long strides. A bareheaded Jackson zipped up his jacket as he came, and Liz felt her pulse accelerate.

She smiled to herself, then flung open the door before he had time to knock.

"I hope it's not too late to stop in," he said as he stamped snow from his feet. He regarded her curiously through eyes that always reminded Liz of a golden autumn. "Are you all right?"

Liz squelched an impulse to move toward him and instead nodded vigorously. "I'm fine—and I'm glad you came by. The girls just left. We were tying up loose ends for the Valentine's Day party and quilt auction." She held out her arm for his coat. "Come on in. There's coffee in the kitchen—and I'll bring out the rest of Mary Ann's apple pie."

She led the way from the foyer and past the library. With her guests tucked away on the second and third floors, they could talk privately in the comfortable nook adjacent to the kitchen. Sarah had left the area spotless, and when Liz turned on the light, it illuminated an arrangement of yellow and orange limonium. The flowers were among her favorites since they could last up to fourteen days in a vase.

Jackson stood while she poured coffee into two china mugs, waiting for her to sit before taking a chair across from her. He looked briefly into the rising steam, then said, "Chief Houghton caught me up on what happened. Liz, I'm really sorry."

The tenderness in his voice could make her cry if she wasn't careful. "Yes, it's an awful thing. Not what you expect to see on a quiet winter morning." She looked down, remembering that Jackson had been there the day before and brought the table he had refinished for her. At the time she had been praising the handsome O'Rourke who had just restored heat to the inn, and had been so mesmerized by the man that she'd barely even thanked Jackson for his trouble. "I . . . uh . . . really love the table you refinished. It's truly beautiful. Thank you."

"My pleasure," Jackson said with a look of satisfaction. His expression sobered as he fixed his hazel eyes on hers. "The chief says Mr. O'Rourke likely had a string of aliases and has been a guest of the state from time to time," he continued. "They're looking into his past arrests and acquaintances—in prison and out. So far, all we've gathered is that he was involved in real estate in one way or another prior to his prison sentence. He was released some months ago and has kept a pretty low profile. It may not be easy to trace his movements since leaving prison and before he came here."

Liz sighed again, remembering Shane O'Rourke when he'd first arrived. *So much for first impressions.* "But he seemed so . . . so nice." She felt her cheeks grow warm, remembering how she had entertained the thought that Jackson might be jealous of her handsome guest. "Just proves the old adage about a book and its cover," she said softly.

Jackson's eyes took on that half-brooding stare that meant he was thinking. He was more than a smart businessman; he was mayor of Pleasant Creek, a town he loved and worked hard to protect and nourish. He shook his head. "Sorry this had to spoil your week with your guests. How are they doing?"

"Well, we're not going to let this spoil *their* vacation. Sadie and Mary Ann kept the Holmes sisters distracted today with quilting. They seem okay. At least they're not talking about wanting to go home—even if they could. The chief made it clear no one was to leave. And they're excited about an Amish shopping trip tomorrow."

"And the birdman?" A shadow appeared in Jackson's eyes. "I understand he found the body and spent a good part of the day answering questions."

It was clear from his tone that Jackson had found something unsavory about the eccentric Felix Horner. Still, Liz knew he would never look down on someone just because he was different.

"Yes. He was pretty upset—as you can imagine—but he made the 911 call and told the police everything he could. Says he didn't know O'Rourke." She hesitated, unsure how to describe Felix. "He really is quite pleasant." She shrugged her shoulders. "He's not letting this affect his winter bird-watching tour. He likes to draw too. When he came down to coffee hour, he brought along a drawing of nuthatches on a snow-covered limb. Not bad."

"I guess no one will be ruled out until the case is solved. It'll be pretty tough, though, with no witnesses to the shooting, no weapon, and no motive." He rubbed a hand over his jaw—a sign that something troubled him. "No motive that we know of," he finished, catching Liz's eye. After a moment he asked quietly. "Does Naomi have an explanation for her photo being found on his body?"

Liz let her breath out slowly. "He's an old boyfriend, apparently still carrying a torch for her. She knew him as Trevor Winston. Guess he was good to her for a while when she was going through a difficult time, but she stopped seeing him ten years ago."

Liz believed what she was saying about Naomi but couldn't deny a niggling doubt in the back of her mind. There had to be something more that Naomi was holding back. But what was it and why?

Jackson pushed aside his mug. "I should be going." He stood but made no move to walk away. "I—I just wanted to make sure you're okay. You will be careful, right?"

"Of course." She smiled, touched that he might be worried about her.

"If there's anything you need—any problems . . ." He broke off, but the anxiety was clear in his expression. "I'm sure the police will keep a close watch . . ." He seemed to be trying to convince himself rather than her. "And I'm just a call away."

Liz stood too; they were side by side, but neither moved. She heard the ticking of the clock on the wall and her own not quite even breathing. She touched his arm, felt the heat of it through his shirt, and quickly removed her hand. "I'll be fine," she said softly, stepping away, "but I'm glad you're looking out for me."

She watched him go, feeling lighter than she had all day. *He's a good friend*, she told herself. *I know he's here for me.* As he would be for all of Pleasant Creek's citizens. Or had he been saying more with those inscrutable hazel eyes? *Don't go there, Liz!*

And she wouldn't. Besides, she was too tired to think clearly. She dimmed the foyer lights and made her way to her quarters.

7

"Thanks for going with me, Sadie," Liz said as she wriggled into her coat. "I've been wanting to visit my neighbors. I see Orpah Hausen occasionally in town, but you don't really get to know a person until you meet them in their own home."

"I'm afraid the Hausens take some getting to know," Sadie said, securing the football-shaped buttons on her long tan coat. "They're not what you would call outgoing—especially Ephraim. He's a real sourpuss." She gave her short white locks a shake and let her breath out in a sigh. "We'll be lucky to get past the front door."

"I have a good reason to go there," Liz said thoughtfully. "Orpah Hausen and I met when Naomi and I were coming home from visiting her mother at Serenity Arms. It wasn't the most ideal circumstance. Naomi was driving and didn't see the Hausens' buggy coming around the corner. Thank God we didn't crash, but it was a close call. She said she was okay, but I'd like to be certain she's all right."

She paused, remembering the blonde girl in high-heeled boots and brilliant red coat who had jumped down from the buggy, shouting at them. Liz hadn't been able to get that red flash out of her mind. Had Rachel been out that morning when O'Rourke was killed?

"There was a young girl with Mrs. Hausen," Liz said. She hurried to keep pace with Sadie's long strides as they walked down the porch steps. Sadie could outwalk and outwork any of the Material Girls. Widowed, she still managed—though on a smaller scale—the farm she and her husband had owned for forty years.

"She said she was her daughter," Liz continued. "But the girl definitely wasn't Amish. And she didn't hold back her opinion of Naomi's driving when she jumped out of the buggy, blonde hair flying in the wind and her eyelashes coated with gobs of mascara."

"Rachel," Sadie supplied knowingly. "She always was a difficult child. And Ephraim was far too hard on her. Didn't want her seeing boys, which for the Amish involves nothing more daring than riding to church or to the singing. Kept her close to the house, and a cheerless place it was from all I've heard. When she was sixteen she left Pleasant Creek for her Rumschpringe."

Liz knew she was referring to a "running around" period when some Amish youth experience greater freedom, a rite of passage when usual behavioral restrictions are relaxed, so that Amish youths can acquire some knowledge of the non-Amish world.

"During Rumschpringe, they're no longer under the control of their parents and, because they are not baptized, they are not yet under the authority of the church." Sadie stopped at the bottom of the porch stairs to zip up her left boot. "I think Rachel has been staying with an aunt in Chicago. Once or twice she's come back for a visit, but it's been a while." Sadie pursed her lips in an ironic grin. "From your description it sounds like she's not ready to take the vows of the church yet."

Liz recalled the pouty mouth, the angry gray eyes beneath a swirl of yellow hair. "No, I don't suppose so." What had gone on in the family or church dynamic that had brought on the breach? There were things a person couldn't know or understand, of course, and she couldn't help thinking back to the events that had led to her own mother's departure from the Amish life. "It's sad," she said with a sigh.

"Come on," Sadie said. "I'll drive."

"In the van?" Liz asked with a sweeping gesture at the gaudy vehicle parked at the curb. The Material Girls called it the "Patchwork Bomb," more for the rise they could get out of Sadie than for any other reason.

The colorful and often-repaired van used to transport supplies for the fabric shop wore a generous blanket of snow, camouflaging its many abrasions. *Definitely an improvement*, Liz thought.

"All right. We'll take my Jeep," Sadie said with mock offense. She glanced back at the parked van. "And what's wrong with the colorful and highly efficient vehicle we all know and love?" she demanded.

"Nothing. Absolutely nothing," Liz said innocently. "But our Amish neighbors might not take kindly to seeing it pull up in front of their plain farmhouse."

"Point taken," Sadie said.

Brilliant rays of sun bounced off the landscape as Liz settled back for the ride. On a nicer day they might have covered the two or three miles on foot, but neither of them had the time or energy to trudge through the snow. The air remained frigid, the wind bone-chilling. The weather could only further impede the investigation into O'Rourke's—or was it Winston's?—death. Footprints had been swiftly covered over during the storm, and temperatures made time of death difficult to pinpoint. The lake was the obvious place to dispose of a gun, but how did authorities go about dragging a frozen body of water if indeed the gun was even there? She forced her gaze away from the forested area where the unthinkable had happened.

An uneventful night of rest had relaxed Liz somewhat. She had served a cheesy egg casserole for her guests, all of whom had seemed in fairly good spirits. Mary Ann had agreed to take Vera and Violet into town for their shopping tour. Felix Horner was going to a wildlife refuge in a nearby village. Their activities had freed her to see what she could learn from the Hausens.

Sadie pulled up to a two-story clapboard house with a slate-gray roof and a tall brick chimney climbing up one side. Like most Amish homes in the area, it was simply constructed with a long front porch, which in summer afforded respite from the day's work. Beyond the house, the typical outbuildings loomed, including a barn faded to sun-bleached dullness. A *Grossdawdy Haus*, or grandparents' house, stood on its own not far from the main dwelling.

"Are there grandparents living there?" Liz asked. She loved the Amish commitment to caring for their elderly. No institutions or rest homes for them; they took care of each other and flourished in a tight-knit cloister of work and worship.

Sadie cut the engine and squinted as she looked out at the bright, empty landscape. No one moved about, nor were there any clothes hanging on the lines upon which blackbirds now perched, silent and unmoving. "No, hasn't been anyone living in the grandparents' house for some time," she said. "Ephraim's parents live with his only brother in Lancaster, Pennsylvania. Orpah's father died some years ago, and only recently her mother succumbed to illness."

"Oh, how difficult for them," Liz murmured, remembering the strained face of Orpah Hausen when she had tried to calm her volatile daughter. "I hope there are children who bring their offspring to fill the house—at least on visits." Most Amish families Liz knew had six or seven children—some had even more.

"There were two sons—twins," Sadie said, her expression darkening. "They died before they were old enough to marry. Both were killed at the tender age of sixteen during their Rumschpringe. They borrowed a car—just wanted to take it for a ride, to see what it was like to drive an English vehicle. Orpah wore only black for a very long time. And Rachel? Well, she was kept close to home under Mutter and *Vater*'s watchful eyes."

Liz knew from her Aunt Ruth and her cousin Miriam that the Amish usually spoke frankly about death, which in their large agricultural communities was a frequent visitor. It was seen as a part of life and as the will of God. Still, of course, the Amish struggled with the same emotions anyone losing a loved one would. She thought of the sons the Hausens had lost.

"That's terrible," Liz said, feeling the dread of tragedy wrap around her. Two sons tragically killed, and then their daughter left home. Rachel with her fancy clothes, her wild, uncovered blonde hair, and heavy eye makeup. No wonder the Hausens mistrusted their English neighbors.

"Rachel was only eight or nine when her brothers died. Orpah had two more children after that, though she was older than most childbearing women. A boy and a girl—probably nine and eleven now. I would say Orpah's into her fifties and Ephraim's a good ten years older." Sadie unlocked her car door. "Rachel was a bit on the wild side, but after the boys died and there were just her parents, she grew even more restless. So you see, I doubt we will be welcomed with open arms. Orpah has her hands full."

Liz shivered as she trudged up to the front porch with Sadie by her side. "I'm glad you're here with me," she said. "At least you have some history with them."

Sadie nodded and rapped on the door. The little alcove in which they stood had a damp, unused feel, as though the front of the house was rarely traversed. It was likely the family used the rear entrance for coming and going between the barn and the house. Sadie stamped her boots on the bristly mat. Liz followed suit, her mind absorbed with the misfortunes of the Hausen family and wishing, at that moment, that no one would be home.

When the door opened a crack, Orpah stood there, anxiety written on her pale features. She seemed closer to sixty than fifty, her ginger hair streaked with gray beneath her Kapp. She wore a plain bluish-gray dress and a long apron of a slightly duller fabric. Wide-spaced gray eyes, not unlike Rachel's—sans mascara—darted from Liz to Sadie and then beyond, as though to see who might be coming behind them.

"Hello, Orpah," Sadie said, giving her a wide smile. "Haven't seen you in a while." She held out a small wrapped parcel. "It's a swatch of fabric from a new line of goods at Sew Welcome," she explained.

Orpah made no move to take it, but she opened the door a bit wider as Sadie pressed the package closer to her. It seemed as though she might refuse the gift, but Sadie hastened on.

"I've brought a friend. You remember Liz Eckardt of the Olde Mansion Inn."

"*Ja*," she said.

Their first meeting had hardly been ideal for generating goodwill. "I'm sorry about the other day," Liz said, "and I wanted to make sure that you're all right."

The wide gray eyes softened a little. Orpah wiped her hands on her apron. She took Sadie's parcel, glanced once again past their shoulders, and nervously gestured for them to enter. "We are all right," she said, moving her lips stiffly as though perhaps they were unused to speech.

The Hausens must know about what's happened. They would have seen the police swarming around the lake and would have been questioned along with all the neighbors. Liz knew the Amish preferred not to deal with the English police; matters of concern were handled by the bishop and elders of their particular *Ordnung*, the German word for order, discipline, or system. With no central church government, each assembly of Amish was autonomous and deferred to its own governing authority.

"Do you want to sit down?" Orpah asked in a small voice, indicating two straight-backed chairs in the spare front room.

A fire bloomed in the fireplace, lessening the austerity of the plain walls and stark furniture. A small table next to an oversized rocking chair held an assortment of solid-colored fabric pieces, which their host might have been working on when she had been interrupted. The familiar aroma of bread emanated from the kitchen, but no voices filled the silent house. There was no sign of Rachel or of anyone else at home. The two younger children were probably in school or outside doing their chores.

She scanned the plain room, particularly the coats and cloaks that hung from pegs just inside the sitting room. The red coat Rachel had worn when she jumped angrily from Orpah's buggy was nowhere in sight. *Where was Rachel?* "Thank you," Liz said when they were seated.

No one said anything for several moments, and no suggestion of coffee or refreshment came. From the corner of her eye, she saw Sadie raise an eyebrow; even the indomitable Sadie was at a loss for words.

Just begin, Liz told herself and looked at their hostess directly. She was a pleasingly round woman with a heart-shaped face that Liz thought might once have been beautiful. But lines at her eyes and rippling her forehead spoke of hardship, of discontent.

"Mrs. Hausen, did you notice anything unusual yesterday? I mean, before the police came—someone walking behind your house in the early morning or . . ." Liz paused. "You see, the man who died was a guest at the inn and—"

"We already spoke with your police," Orpah interrupted. "We did not see anything; we were busy with our work. We know nothing about that man who . . ." She let the rush of words fall away and looked down at her hands, which fluttered like nervous birds in her lap.

"I'm sorry to trouble you," Liz said patiently. "But we need to know what happened, why Mr. O'Rourke was killed." Why is Orpah so nervous? Is it simply discomfort over the painful subject of murder or is it entertaining Englishers in her home? Or could it be something else?

"These matters don't concern us." Orpah bit down on her lip that had started to tremble. "We wish only to be left alone to do our work . . ."

Sadie's voice broke in calmly but firmly. "But when someone is hurt or in trouble, surely it's everyone's concern."

Tears filled the woman's eyes. The Amish believed in the Bible's injunction to care for one's neighbor, to give comfort to the ailing. Doubtless, Orpah accepted that, but sorrow had a way of turning the sufferer inward. Liz thought of the twin boys who had wanted only to feel the rush of an engine propelling them across the countryside. Boys Orpah Hausen had nurtured and then buried in the cold, unyielding ground.

She stood and took a few steps toward Orpah. "I'm grateful that you and your daughter weren't hurt." She paused, waited for the eyes to connect with hers. "Is Rachel here?" she asked hesitantly. "I would like to talk to her."

"*Nay*, my *Töchter* is not here." Orpah let her breath out in a slow sigh. "That is, she is not in this house. She is staying in the Grossdawdy Haus . . . but she knows nothing that would be useful. She . . ."

A door opened noisily, and a hulking figure appeared in the space between the kitchen and the sitting room. A huge man in dark pants and suspenders, a plain work shirt, and boots stood scowling at them. A black felt coat hung from his wide shoulders, bits of straw clinging to the fabric. Thick gray hair stuck out wildly on his head and meshed with a bushy beard that fell to his chest. His eyes were angry coals in his weathered face. He looked like a vengeful prophet about to call on God to destroy the infidels.

Liz drew in her breath.

"Ephraim, these ladies have come to visit," Orpah began in a trembling voice. "You know Mrs. Schwarzentruber. *Und* this is Miss Eckardt from the inn. They—they ask about the Englisher who . . ." Her voice fell away under the harsh glare of her husband.

He was obviously displeased at their presence in his home, but he retained the appearance of good manners intrinsic to the Amish and managed a courteous nod. But his big hands remained curled into fists at his sides. "We know about the Englisher," he said, muting a voice as powerful as his frame. "But it does not concern us. Your police have already been here. We wish to be left to our work."

"Mr. Hausen," Liz began politely, "we're sorry to bother you . . ." A lump caught in her throat.

Undoubtedly, he had seen Sadie's car draw up to the house while out working in the barn or feeding the animals and had come to chase them away. *A real sourpuss,* Sadie had said, warning that they would not find a warm welcome. She had been right.

Liz squared her shoulders. "We are trying to help—to find out what happened. Your wife was kind enough to speak with us, but we would like to talk to your daughter or anyone who might have seen or heard something."

"Rachel has nothing to tell you." A hard edge sharpened the name on his lips. "We have nothing more to say. Now I must ask you to leave this house in peace. Bitte." Never had those syllables sounded more threatening.

Liz felt her pulse racing; her tongue seemed frozen.

Orpah abruptly lifted her guests' coats from the pegs along the wall. She opened the door for them to retrieve their boots that were stored just outside on the mat. "It is best if you leave now," she whispered. "I'm sorry." She spread her hands in a helpless gesture. "I thank you for the fabric. It was kind of you."

Liz and Sadie glanced across at Ephraim Hausen, who stood glowering in the doorway as they put on their coats. He looked as if he intended to remain there like a fierce sentinel until he heard their car's engine bear his unwelcome visitors away.

8

"It's rare to hear a cardinal sing in winter, but I'm almost sure I heard a female yesterday." Felix Horner pursed his lips in a whirring whistle that began low and ascended in pitch. "When it's a duet, the female sings first, then the male answers with a punctuated *chip-chip-chip*. It's really quite amazing." Horner's eyes glistened as he sat at the table, the ever-present binoculars riding the small curve of his stomach.

"Oh, Felix!" Violet gushed. "How do you do that?" She puckered her lips and tried to imitate the sounds but broke off laughing. "I'm sure I'll never master it."

"Most of us would do a good deal better to master the English language," Vera said with a disapproving edge to her voice. She twitched her nose as though she smelled something unpleasant. "Pass me some of that egg concoction, if you please."

Liz handed the dish to her left where Violet sat dressed in her signature purple—today a ruffled blouse and matching cardigan. The night's rest had been refreshing once Liz had been able to put out of her mind the previous day's unsettling visit to the Hausen farm. It was good to sit in the dining room with her guests enjoying the breakfast she and Sarah had prepared.

"Some very interesting birds were showcased at the wildlife refuge," Felix went on, passing the casserole to Vera without helping himself to more. "Quite a serviceable collection of birds and habitat," he continued. "Mind you, it was nothing as grand as my Annabelle Aviary would . . ." He frowned, and a coldness washed the sparkle from his eyes. Presently, he looked up in surprise, as though he'd been caught thinking out loud and wondered exactly what he had said.

Annabelle Aviary. *That has an alliterative ring*, Liz thought.

The bird-watcher brightened. "Did you know that the song of a Eurasian wren is made of more than seven hundred different notes a minute and can be heard over a thousand feet away?"

"Remarkable," Liz responded to the man's enthusiasm. She was careful to keep a straight face as he shook the comical fringe of fawn-colored hair that dipped over his forehead. When he removed his wire-rimmed glasses to wipe them with his as-yet-unused napkin, she was surprised to see how small his blue-gray eyes actually were when not magnified by the lenses. Small and startling somehow. She was glad when he put his spectacles back on.

Apparently he had forgotten the messy business of their guest's demise and even the extensive interrogation and search he'd been subjected to. Which was why Liz was dismayed when Vera brought the subject up.

The elderly lady briefly touched her napkin to her lips and addressed her question to Liz. "Has the investigation revealed any new clues relating to that man's death?"

It was awkward to call him by name—since he apparently had used several aliases over time. Perhaps referring to him simply as "that man" made him seem less real, easier to forget. Liz sighed. A life had been summarily cut off; he should at least have a name. "If Mr. O'Rourke was here in Pleasant Creek for some particular reason it may not have been a good one," she said. "Given what the police have learned of his background. He had a prison record."

"But he seemed so pleasant and helpful," Violet cooed. She shook her silver curls and frowned into her still-heaping plate. The kindhearted Violet seemed genuinely sad.

"Well, I heard that that woman from the bakery has a close connection," Vera said. "She might be the one who offed him."

Liz was startled, not only by the uncharacteristic language that fell from Vera's lips, but by realizing that gossip about Naomi had spread, even to guests at the inn.

Violet paused in mid-bite. "Not that sweet Naomi Mason who helped me with my quilt during our first visit here! I was so touched by her kindness."

"Violet, dear, you are gullible to a fault," Vera said without rancor. "But the most pleasant face can hide a sinister mind, you know."

Sarah, who had stepped in with fresh coffee, said nothing. But her body language clearly showed her disapproval of the idle talk about Naomi.

Liz felt her stomach tighten. "Naomi knew Mr. O'Rourke, but that doesn't mean she . . ." Liz looked from one face to the other as the twins bantered back and forth. Only Felix remained silent, separating the casserole from the sausage links on his plate. "Naomi has no reason to want him dead," Liz said in what she hoped was an unbiased tone. "It's much more likely that one of his old cohorts killed him." She shifted in her chair. "Besides, Chief Houghton is satisfied with Naomi's alibi; she was at the bakery all morning. Her coworker vouches for her—as will any of the early customers."

An uncomfortable silence ensued, but suddenly Felix jumped and pushed back from the table, uttering a startled protest in sharp syllables. "Great jumping Jehoshaphat!"

Beans huffed and scooted out from under the table, looking disgruntled.

"What is that animal doing under there?" Felix sputtered.

Beans had been stretched out in a patch of sunlight by the sideboard, but apparently he had slouched beneath the table and chosen to plop himself on top of the little man's feet.

"Sorry!" Liz said, steeling herself against the urge to laugh. "Go lie down," she charged the dog in her severest tone, pointing to the kitchen.

Sometimes Beans could be completely maddening. Of all people to bestow his bulk upon, why would he choose a man who clearly disliked dogs—a fact Felix had made abundantly clear the first time they had met?

Felix sat down again, settling the displaced binoculars and clearing his throat. "I do apologize for my outburst. I didn't realize the beast was under there." He struggled to rearrange his facial features into a more acceptable alignment, but the red flush in his cheeks remained. His magnified eyes were huge and far from warm. "You've no idea what our feathered friends suffer from animals like—well, I don't mean to say dogs are the biggest threat . . ." He cleared his throat once more. "Did you know that in the continental U.S. alone, between one point four and three point seven billion birds are killed by cats annually?" He stood up as though to depart.

"Beans is entirely harmless," Liz said, suppressing a grin. Felix should be glad that Beans was simply a mild-mannered bulldog and not a feisty cat ready to pounce on him at the first trill of a mimicked birdcall. "I'm so sorry he startled you. I'll make sure he doesn't invade your space again—especially at mealtime."

Without a reply, Felix turned and left the dining room. When the footsteps on the stairs receded into silence, indicating that Felix was gone, Liz said, "He really is fond of his birds, isn't he?"

Violet turned her attention back from the window where Liz could see Stefan scattering ice melt over the walkway to the back door, his bright red knitted tuque pulled over his abundant hair. "I suppose he does," Vera said with a little laugh.

"Was he like that as a child?" Liz asked mildly. She was referring to Felix, but her attention, too, had been diverted. Perhaps Stefan and Violet were sweet on each other, though to her knowledge they were barely acquainted. Quickly her nervous concern over Stefan's whereabouts the morning the body had been found returned to plague her.

"Actually, we have no idea what Felix was like," Vera answered for her sister. She sat back in her chair and folded her arms over her gray wool jacket to which a cameo brooch was pinned. "He lived in Chicago. We grew up in Pennsylvania. I'm afraid our parents didn't mix much with his family. Our family was very small. Father was an only child and Mother had one sister—Felix's mother." She pursed her lips. "Felix and his mother never seemed to need anyone else but each other."

Liz furrowed her brow. *What a strange comment*, Liz thought.

"We always felt sad not to know them," Violet ruminated. "But there was that one summer when we were teenagers." She looked off into the distance, recalling old memories. "Mother drove Sister and me all the way to Chicago when Aunt Annabelle came down with influenza. We stayed a whole week while Mother cared for her sister, but after that summer, Mother never spoke about our aunt or Felix again."

"So when he called out of the blue a few weeks ago, you could have knocked us over with a feather." Vera grimaced. "An apt metaphor in this instance, don't you think?"

"We chatted on and on like we'd been friends all our lives," Violet chimed in. "When we told him we were coming here for a vacation he got quite excited. One thing led to another, and we suggested he might like to come to the Olde Mansion Inn too—and well, here we all are."

Vera made a harrumphing sound and shrugged her shoulders. "But I'm still not getting up to watch birds at the crack of dawn." She pushed back her chair. "Sister, are you coming? We have a date at Sew Welcome. Sadie said she would show us that new quilt pattern." She turned on her sensible heels. "And Sadie had better not forget her promise!"

Liz watched them go, mystified by the strange weavings of life. Two sisters apparently set in their ways, an eccentric bird-watcher, an ex-con, and a lawyer-turned-innkeeper. What circumstances brought these particular people to this place at this time in history?

When Beans poked his head warily into the room, she patted her knee, inviting him in. She scratched his bristly head. "Well, it's just you and me, buddy," she said with a sigh.

"And me," Sarah said, sailing in to retrieve the breakfast dishes. "But didn't you tell me you were going to work on decorations for the Valentine's Day party today?"

"I did," Liz said, giving Beans a final pat. "Naomi and I will work in the back room at the bakery so she can keep an eye out for customers." She had confirmed it with a call before going to bed the night before. That Naomi hadn't been her usual convivial self was easily understood in light of the investigation and the trailing whispers. *Perhaps I can get her mind off things with a little art project.*

"You go on," Sarah said, smiling. "I can finish up here. I know the decorations will be beautiful. And tell Miss Mason . . ." She twisted the strings of her Kapp and lowered her eyes. "Tell Miss Mason we are praying for her."

Liz smiled and waited for her gaze to return. "I'll tell her," she said softly. Sweet Sarah, for whom faith was a living, everyday reality. "Now, put your head out the back door and ask Stefan to come around. I have the decoration supplies in boxes at the front door; I'll need him to help me get them over to the bakery. And have him bring the serving cart—the one on wheels."

———————— //////////////////////////// ————————

She covered the short distance to the bakery with Stefan pushing and her pulling the cart over the shoveled walk. She held the front door open for him and saw with some dismay that the little white tables were all but empty—empty except for the one table near the center of the room where Naomi sat, staring into space.

At the sound of the tinkling bell Naomi stood and brushed off her apron. "Hi," she said and gestured for Stefan to take the cart through to the back. She looked despairingly around the café area and turned to Liz. "I suppose we could work in here. There's not much going on . . . as you can see."

Liz's heart sank at the sight of the empty tables and the dark circles under her friend's eyes. "Give them time; your customers will come around," she said softly.

"The only ones to 'come around' were two strangers and Edie Huffington, who probably wouldn't have come if she hadn't had unexpected company." Naomi straightened the green turtleneck beneath her apron and tucked back a strand of hair that had strayed from her chignon. She gave a wry smile. "Never mind. Let's go back and see what your crafty mind has cooked up."

When Stefan hefted one of the boxes onto the table, Liz couldn't help noticing that the effort left him slightly breathless. The glass vases for the centerpieces were heavy, she knew. But before she could say anything, Stefan finished unloading and left, dragging the noisy cart after him.

Naomi drew an assortment of craft paper in shades of red and pink from a second box and stacked it on the worktable, which she had covered with a protective cloth. She pulled out an enormous bag of candy from the carton. "I suppose these conversation hearts are for us to snack on while we work?"

"I think not," Liz said, glad that Naomi's sense of humor hadn't entirely vanished. "Believe it or not, they're for the centerpieces. Each vase will hold a four-inch-diameter candle like this one." She unwrapped a white pillar and set it inside the vase. "Then we take a couple handfuls of the candy hearts and cluster them around the candle. Top it all off with a ribbon like this one . . ." She pulled out a length of wire-edged ribbon in a lustrous shade of pink and tied it at the middle of the glass vase. "Voilà!"

"Simple but elegant. You're a genius," Naomi said.

Liz sighed. "Actually I got it off the Internet. I found a clever website that has more ideas than Carter has pills." She smiled. "Does Carter still manufacture pills?"

Naomi grinned and continued unpacking the supplies Liz had brought. After a few moments working silently, Naomi said, "Is Stefan all right? I noticed he looked a little pale."

"I noticed that too." Liz frowned. "He's been doing a lot of shoveling." *And disappearing for a while.* But she'd found him to be trustworthy—as Jackson had—and he worked harder than two men. Not only that, but it really wasn't any of her business where he went. "I'll have to get him to slow down a bit. At least the snow has finally stopped. I was beginning to think we'd taken a wrong turn into Antarctica."

They finished making the centerpieces and began working on garlands to hang around the hall at the Otter Lodge. She had chosen to make a simple heart chain, using four paper strips at a time, two of which were folded outward to form the next heart in the chain. Stored loosely in large trash bags, the garlands could be preserved and hung later to provide a big splash of color without a lot of expense.

"Is everything going along okay for the auction?" Naomi asked, stapling the end of a long chain of hearts. "I'm sorry I couldn't come to the last meeting. The Material Girls will think I've abandoned them." She was silent for several seconds before adding, "I haven't started the frosted heart cookies I promised yet, but I will." She sat down heavily. "Guess my heart hasn't been in it—no pun intended."

"All the girls send their love," Liz said quietly. "This has been so hard on you."

"I think one of Houghton's officers has been following me. Makes me so nervous to be watched like a criminal." She pressed down hard on the stapler. "And the gossip behind my back . . ."

"Oh, Naomi." Liz shook her head slowly. *What can I say that will help?* "Sarah wanted me to tell you she's praying for you. We're all concerned, but we'll get to the bottom of it."

Tears welled up in Naomi's gentle brown eyes. "I'm sorry. I thought I was all cried out by now."

"Naomi, let's go get a cup of coffee," Liz suggested. "We'll sit at one of your cheery tables in the café and try to relax. You've worked hard enough."

"You want anything to eat?" Naomi asked when they were seated.

"No, coffee's fine," Liz said. Quietness reigned, broken only by the ticking of the white-rimmed clock with pink tulips for hour and minute hands. They couldn't avoid the subject that was on both their minds. What had happened out there by the lake? Who had killed the man carrying Naomi's picture? "Naomi, you did tell the chief you knew Trevor Winston, didn't you?"

"Yes, right after you left." She bit her trembling lip. "And I had to identify his body. It was awful . . . seeing him like that."

"I'm sorry," Liz said gently.

"I never expected to see him again. I never wanted to." Something smoldered behind her dark eyes. She cupped her hands around her mug of coffee, and Liz saw that she was shivering. "In the beginning he was good to me, and I needed someone to care about me. But the relationship ended a long time ago. He was always into some money-making scheme, and there were other girls. Lots of them. It was hard to accept that it was my money he was interested in."

Yes, the wealthy Mason family. Liz thought of Moriah, Naomi's mother, living in the top-notch senior care facility, of the expensive clothing and furnishings in her spacious suite. Of Naomi's cash purchase of the bakery. *So O'Rourke/Winston was a parasite who preyed on wealthy women.* "He didn't write to you or try to call in ten years?" Liz asked. "And you have no idea what he wanted after all this time?"

She hadn't meant to ask the question. Even in her own ears it sounded like an interrogation, and hadn't Naomi already answered these questions—both hers and those of Chief Houghton? She looked up and saw hurt in her friend's eyes. Hurt and something else. Fear?

"No. I already told the police. They don't believe me, but I thought my best friend would." She stared down into her mug again.

Suddenly there was a swift tinkling of the bell as the door to the bakery flew open. Rachel Hausen came charging toward their table, crimson coat flapping open, high-heeled boots beating a sharp tattoo on the tile floor. Her eyes were wild, her angry red face streaked with tears. "It was you!" she shrilled, rushing at Naomi. "You killed him!"

9

"You killed him!" Rachel shrieked again. She flung herself at Naomi and pummeled her with fists encased in bulky striped mittens.

"No!" Naomi gasped, staring into the small red face pressed up to hers, eyes wide with shock. "Who? What do you—?"

"Stop!" Liz pushed in between them and forced Rachel back. Rachel was a petite girl, easily held at bay. She continued to flail her arms.

"Why couldn't you just give him what he wanted?" she screamed at Naomi as she tried to wrest her arms free from Liz's grasp. "You didn't have to kill him!"

"Just stop it, Rachel," Liz repeated. "Settle down." She pushed the girl toward a chair. "We will talk like adults—unless you'd rather I phone the police."

The girl turned her tear-streaked face to Liz, and recognition seemed to dawn. It had only been a few days since her mother's buggy had nearly collided with Naomi's car. Rachel backed up and swiped at her flushed face with a mittened hand. Then, collapsing into the chair, she burst into full-blown sobs.

Liz searched Naomi's face. "Do you know this girl?" Liz asked over Rachel's sobs.

"I know she's the Hausens' daughter, but I . . ."

Liz had been present for their encounter on the road between the Serenity Arms nursing home and the Olde Mansion Inn. But had Naomi and Rachel been acquainted before?

Naomi shook her head violently. "What is she doing here, saying that I—"

Rachel raised her face from her hands. "Shane didn't do anything wrong; he wouldn't . . ." she sputtered. The weeping took over, swallowing her words.

Liz reached for a napkin from the colorful holder that graced each of the café tables and held it toward Rachel. "So you knew Shane O'Rourke, or Trevor Winston, that is," she said in an even, controlled voice. No one got that upset over someone she didn't know. But Rachel, the wayward daughter of a respected Amish family? What did she have to do with someone like him?

"Shane was . . ." She struggled to explain. "He was my friend. I—I loved him!" she burst out, glaring at Naomi. "You had no right to kill him."

Naomi continued to shake her head—in wonder or denial, Liz couldn't tell.

"Listen, Rachel," Liz began firmly. "The gossip you've been listening to is false. The police have questioned Naomi and confirmed her alibi. She was right here working in the bakery and nowhere near the place where Mr. O'Rourke . . ." She broke off, visualizing anew the handsome face, the bloodstained snow. "Naomi wasn't there." She paused to underscore her words, then held Rachel's gaze. "You, on the other hand, were at your parents' place—very near the woods where the man was found."

Liz waited for her words to sink in. She might have added that she had seen someone running—someone wearing red. Red like Miss Rachel Hausen's fashionable coat.

Rachel's face, still wet and blotched, turned ashen. "I didn't kill him. I couldn't. I loved him!" she cried. "We were going to meet in the woods across from the farm. But the police were there—and Shane was . . ." Another paroxysm of weeping drowned her words.

"Why was he here, Rachel? What was he doing in Pleasant Creek?"

It couldn't be a coincidence that the two of them showed up at roughly the same time. Rachel had been with her mother in the afternoon on a quiet country road. O'Rourke or Winston had appeared at the inn a few hours later. Liz's mind whirled as she tried to make sense of it all. "What did he want from Naomi?" she asked sternly. "What was it you think she should have given your—friend?"

Rachel had pulled off the striped mittens and thrown them on the floor where they lay abandoned. She wiped at her face with delicate hands and looked from Liz to Naomi with enormous, wide-spaced eyes. "I don't know!" she wailed. "I don't know!"

"You must know," Liz said. "You must know a great deal more than you're saying."

"I only know that Shane is dead—and it's all because of her!" She jabbed a red-tipped finger at Naomi.

Naomi seemed too shocked to object. Tight-lipped and pale, she shook her head until the bell over the bakery door announced a patron.

Two well-dressed women unknown to Liz entered, chatting as they advanced toward the untended counter. They appeared not to notice the little group near the back of the room.

Naomi got up and robotically headed toward the counter. Rachel huddled inside her coat and turned her face to the window. Liz swiveled in the chair to avoid eye contact with the customers—perhaps the only customers who hadn't heard the local chin-wag and hadn't absented themselves from the bakery.

When Naomi was out of earshot, Liz said, "Look, Rachel, this is no place to talk. But we've got to sort this out. Will you let me take you home? To your parents."

"No! No!" Rachel whispered fiercely. "Vater won't—"

Obviously, Rachel knew what Liz had been told in no uncertain terms: She wasn't welcome at the Hausen farm. "We can go next door to my house to talk in private," Liz coaxed. When Rachel continued to sniff and shake her head in refusal, Liz surprised herself by saying, "You can talk to me—or talk to Chief Houghton. You choose."

Rachel hesitated, sniffed back more tears, and finally nodded. She blew her nose, her face still turned away from the counter.

The two matrons, oblivious to the momentous confrontation going on, continued to exclaim over delectable-looking treats in the glass case. Studiously ignoring the two people at the far table, Naomi bagged the purchases the customers chose.

Liz stood and ushered Rachel toward the door. "Wait for me right outside," she told the girl.

Rachel appeared completely deflated now, the blonde curls limp on the shoulders of her red coat. Ignoring her mittens, she walked slowly to the door while Liz turned to catch Naomi's eye.

She mouthed the words, "I'll call you later" and tried to reassure Naomi with her eyes.

Liz's pulse raced with the shock of the last few moments. Not only had Rachel Hausen been in the general area where Shane O'Rourke, alias Trevor Winston, was killed: she *knew* him. Had she shot him in a jealous rage? The idea of the diminutive Rachel with a gun in her hand seemed ludicrous. Even more unbelievable was the notion that the slight young woman could drag a man's body up an incline to the wooded section along the lake all by herself. But what more did she know, and what would it mean for Naomi?

"Would you like a cup of tea or hot chocolate?" Liz asked when she and Rachel were alone in Liz's private sitting room. They'd gone in the back door of the inn, avoiding traffic areas.

Rachel gave a negative shake of her head without looking up at Liz. She had relinquished the red coat and boots before following Liz into her quarters and now obediently sank down in the chair Liz had indicated. She looked small and forlorn in an oversized pink sweater and skinny jeans—the kind that likely gave her staid Amish parents fits. In spite of her pallor, she glowed with youth and more beauty than was probably good for her.

"How old are you, Rachel?" Liz asked.

"Twenty-one my last birthday," she said in a dull voice as she laced and unlaced fingers that glistened with red polish.

"How long have you been away from home?"

Rachel moistened her bow-shaped lips with the tip of her tongue. "When I was sixteen I went to Chicago to stay with my aunt." She moved uncomfortably in the upholstered chair and went on. "She's not Amish. She owns a flower shop. She kept saying I should go home, but I . . ." She stopped, rearranged her legs. "I came home every few months to see Mutter . . ." She broke off at the Amish reference to her mother. "It makes her happy, but Vater . . ." Her delicate brow wrinkled and her chin trembled.

Liz felt a stab of sympathy, recalling the unbending Ephraim Hausen and Sadie's assessment of Rachel's cheerless childhood years. In their sorrow over losing their boys, had the Hausens overprotected Rachel or made life so miserable that she had to get away? And what would be the fate of the two younger children?

Liz steeled herself, intent on getting some answers from the troubled young woman. "Tell me about Mr. O'Rourke."

Rachel winced as though his name was painful to hear. She fidgeted some more and leaned forward so that her elbows rested on her knees. "He—he said he loved me." She was quiet for what seemed a long time, then picked up her account of her dashing boyfriend. They had met at the restaurant where she worked as a waitress. "He said we were perfect for each other."

"How long did you know him?" Liz asked.

She gave a rebellious shrug of her shoulders and clamped her mouth shut. Then, reconsidering, she said softly, "A couple of months, I guess. He was . . ." She stopped and began to grow agitated. "But my aunt didn't approve. She wouldn't let me bring him to her house, so I got a room over the restaurant where I worked. We were going to go away—be together after . . ."

"After he got what he wanted in Pleasant Creek?" Liz finished for her.

After a long moment, Rachel looked up. "It's not true!" she shouted. "What that policeman said about Shane can't be true."

"Did he tell you that he had been in prison for fraud and assault? That he went by a number of aliases and—"

"Stop." She put her hands over her ears like a small child would. "I don't want to hear it."

"It's a matter of record, Rachel. You must know that." Liz waited as the girl rocked vigorously in the chair, head bent low over her lap. "Rachel, you need to tell me why Shane came here to Pleasant Creek. What was it he wanted from Naomi?"

She stopped rocking; her shoulders slumped against the chair. "He wouldn't tell me. He . . . he had a picture and asked if I knew her. I recognized the lady who bought the bakery. I told him she lived in the same town as my parents." She put both hands to her temples. "I shouldn't have told him. If we hadn't come here, Shane would still be alive."

"Why was he looking for her?" Liz urged.

"He said he knew her from a long time ago, that she had something he needed." She bit down hard on her lip. "But he wouldn't tell me what it was." She drew in a deep breath and let it out in a huff. "Why did he have to come here? Now he's dead. I'll never see him again." She got up suddenly and made for the door. "I've got to go."

Liz watched with sadness and frustration as Rachel grabbed her coat and fled onto the porch where she jammed her feet into her boots. Wrapping herself into the red coat, she ran quickly away, leaving the vague scent of cheap rose perfume in her wake.

There seemed nothing more Rachel could tell her. Whatever O'Rourke or Winston had wanted from Naomi would remain a mystery.

Unless Naomi knew what he was after and for some reason refused to reveal it.

10

The next day after cleaning up from breakfast at the inn, Liz joined the Material Girls in Sew Welcome's workroom. Sadie, Mary Ann, Opal, and Caitlyn were busy preparing for the quilt auction and Valentine's Day party. Time was growing short to finish all the details involved in the large community event to benefit the hospital.

"Anyone seen the staple gun?" Sadie said, pushing aside a confusion of papers, ribbon, and fabric scraps. "I need it to attach bid numbers to these." She held up one of the wooden paddles that had been donated by the local paint store.

"On top of that shelf behind you," Opal supplied, stooping to stow her workbag at her feet. Today she had brought no photos for sharing, though amusing stories about her grandchildren flowed with the conversation.

Caitlyn's hair was streaked with cherry red. She had the most intriguing color sense, and her hair was seldom left out of the equation. "You'll be pleased to know that I finished my quilt—finally!" she said in her lyrical, girlish voice that could cheer the gloomiest atmosphere. "But I had to rescue it from Kelly more than once. You'd think being a rescue dog herself she would be more grateful—and sleep with her own blanket!"

The youngest of the Material Girls, Caitlyn was in her late twenties and single. She added a great deal of merriment to the group, particularly with tales of the greyhound she had adopted from the local animal shelter. She was a busy nurse, and her schedule sometimes compromised time for the quilting she loved. Today she had managed some time off to help the Material Girls get ready for the auction. She unfolded her quilt which was done in a Morning Star pattern. The popular design featured an eight-point star that exploded with dizzying color against a galaxy-black background and brilliant tumbling blocks.

"It's gorgeous!" Opal said, touching the bright geometric shapes with her knobby fingers. "If it were mine, I'd be hard-pressed to part with it—even for my sweet Madison Ruby." She leaned back with a fond smile. "Did I tell you that Maddy can say her ABCs perfectly?"

Sadie examined the colorful star quilt, deftly ignoring Madison Ruby's alphabetical prowess. "It's a beauty," she said but allowed only a second or two more for admiration before heading for the cupboard along the wall. She called to Caitlyn over her shoulder, "What? No butter cake today?"

No one baked a butter cake like Caitlyn. Light, fluffy with just a hint of lemon, it was a favorite of all the Material Girls.

"I'm lucky to remember my own name, let alone where my kitchen is these days. Between my ER duties and helping out at the clinic here in town, my life has been a zoo." Caitlyn drew a long-suffering face. "They've been short-staffed, but after this month, the clinic will have someone to replace me."

Sadie was still rummaging through cupboards for supplies, and Opal followed Mary Ann into the back room for coffee, leaving only Caitlyn and Liz at the wide worktable. Together they carefully refolded the quilt. "It really is lovely," Liz said, "and it's sure to bring a good price. Thanks for working so hard."

"You're the one carrying the biggest responsibility for this shindig," Caitlyn said. "Not sure how you do it with the inn to run and everything." Her sparkly red earrings jingled as she shook her head in wonder.

"I love community projects," Liz said. "Especially when they benefit a group in town. As for running the inn, I have lots of help."

"Speaking of help," Caitlyn began, raising an eyebrow, "how is Stefan these days?"

Liz shrugged, mildly surprised. "He's fine but getting a workout with all this snow. You'd think we were in the middle of Siberia—not Indiana."

"I saw him a couple times at the clinic . . ." She paused. "The other day in the parking lot I called out to say hi, but I don't think he heard me."

"Oh?"

"Yes. It was Wednesday, I think." Caitlyn cocked her head and her blue eyes widened. "Yes, the day that man was killed across the lake. Terrible thing."

"What time was that?" Liz asked in what she hoped was an offhand manner.

"About nine—no, exactly nine, because I remember thinking I was going to be late. I had agreed to work on Thursday and Friday only, but that week they were short-staffed on Wednesday, so guess who just hasn't learned to say no?" Caitlyn spread her fingers in a helpless gesture.

Liz didn't know whether to be relieved or anxious. If Stefan had been in the clinic parking lot at nine, it was likely he hadn't been at the lake. But why had he lied? Could Caitlyn have gotten the time wrong?

Sadie, Mary Ann, and Opal returned to the table, and the topic of Stefan ended. No one had asked Liz about her meeting with Naomi the day before, but she had seen the questions in their eyes. Now Mary Ann put down the scissors with an immaculately manicured hand. Dark brown eyes intent on Liz, she asked the question that was on everyone's mind: "Is Naomi okay?"

Liz drew in a breath and let it out slowly. "She's struggling, but she's doing her best to cope in spite of all the tongue-wagging going on." She sighed, remembering the dark shadows under Naomi's eyes, the dejected slump of her shoulders.

"I feel so terrible about this," Mary Ann said softly. "Dredging up the past can be so painful."

Liz was inclined to agree, though dredging up the past had sometimes been healing in her case. It was Mary Ann's long-ago friendship with Abigail Byler, Liz's mother, that had helped Liz find her heritage. When they were young girls, Liz's mother and Mary Ann had worked in the fabric store owned by Mary Ann's family. Many years later, she had been able to connect Liz with her mother's Amish beginnings and with relatives she'd never known existed.

"We need to find out what really happened to Mr. O'Rourke—or whatever his name is," Sadie said, her blue eyes setting off fiery sparks. "You'd think the police would come up with some answers by now."

"Something happened yesterday," Liz began. She took a deep breath as everyone stared. "Rachel Hausen came storming into the bakery while Naomi and I were having coffee, and she accused Naomi of killing her boyfriend."

"Her boyfriend?" Opal dropped the black marker she had been using to number the bid cards. "She knew the dead man? He was her boyfriend?"

Liz nodded, recalling Rachel's angry sobs as she lunged at Naomi and later as she sat in her quarters at the inn. "Yes. She says he came to Pleasant Creek to see Naomi, but she doesn't know why. She knows that they were once friends, and she was angry that he wanted to connect with her. She's terribly jealous."

"A classic motive for murder," Mary Ann said.

Sadie made a harrumphing sound. "Rachel has her faults, and she's done considerable running around, but picking up a gun and shooting a man . . ." She pursed her lips in thought, brows knit tightly. Was Sadie reconsidering the possibility that Rachel could be guilty?

"Have they found the weapon?" Opal wanted to know.

"As far as I've heard, they haven't." Liz said as she brushed an imaginary thread from her woolly sweater. "The heavy snow that morning and the continuing cold makes it hard to gather clues. But the chief is—" She left the sentence unfinished because the door suddenly opened and Stan Houghton himself poked his head inside.

"Sorry to interrupt," he said, removing his cap and revealing a shock of disarrayed hair. He caught Liz's eye. "I need to have a word with you."

"Of course," she said. She got up, glanced briefly at the surprised women around the table, and went to join him. "Carry on," she called over her shoulder.

Once in the foyer, Liz ushered the chief into the sitting room. With the Holmes sisters away attending a matinee at the theater, and Felix Horton off on his usual bird-watching pursuits, the sitting room was vacant. Sarah had lit a fire that burned gently in the grate. "We can talk in here," Liz suggested.

Houghton unbuttoned his coat but made no move to shed it entirely.

"Is anything wrong?" She realized how inane the question sounded. He was hardly here in the middle of the day on a social call. And something certainly *was* wrong. A man had been murdered, and his killer was still at large. The chief had removed his boots at the door, and Liz saw that there was a hole in the toe of his left sock. The picture didn't fit with the profile of a hard-core cop. But any crook mistaking Stan Houghton's humble appearance for haphazard crime fighting was in for a rude awakening.

His burly frame filled the wing chair across from Liz. "There have been some developments that I thought you should know about." He set his cap on the side table and smoothed his graying hair. "We've been passing O'Rourke's mug shot around, and a truck driver out of Warsaw who makes deliveries for Cross Furniture once or twice a month has identified Mr. O'Rourke as the man he picked up on Highway 30 and drove to Pleasant Creek last Monday." He was peering at her closely. "You said he arrived on Tuesday night. Is that correct?"

"Yes, that's the first time any of us saw him—Tuesday, the night before he was killed." She frowned into the chief's sharp eyes.

"Says he picked him and an unidentified man up in Fort Wayne and dropped O'Rourke off here. Driver didn't get a good look but said the man had shaggy red hair that hung beneath a stained cowboy hat. He was slumped down in the seat and wore big sunglasses that covered his face. Didn't talk—left that to the charming and chatty Mr. O'Rourke."

O'Rourke had been alone when he arrived at the inn. "Do you know who the other man was?"

"The truck driver said he dropped off O'Rourke's companion just outside of Dresden and brought O'Rourke on into Pleasant Creek around noon. He couldn't give much of a description of the other man but he picked out a possible look-alike from mug shots of O'Rourke's former inmates. When we find him we may have our killer." He paused. "Or not. Can't rule anyone out yet."

Liz held his gaze, stunned by the news that Shane O'Rourke had been in town a whole day and a half before arriving at the Olde Mansion. What had he been doing during that time? And what had happened to his valise? The police had searched his room but found no personal effects, and only a handkerchief, a few dollars in a nondescript wallet, and the photograph that had been found on his body.

"It's important that we discover what transpired between Monday noon and Wednesday morning when the body was found," Houghton said. "It seems unlikely he could be in town for thirty-six hours and not be seen by someone. We're circulating his picture; I think it's only a matter of time."

"You said there were developments, plural," Liz said thoughtfully. "Was there something else?"

Houghton fidgeted in his chair and cleared his throat. "There is something else. I'm hoping you might be able to help. It, uh, concerns Miss Mason—Naomi." He paused without looking directly at Liz. "We had a look at her bank records—with a warrant of course."

Liz drew in her breath. *Naomi would be devastated. More embarrassment and intrusion.*

"It seems she withdrew five thousand dollars on Tuesday morning, along with a valuable ring from a safety deposit box. But she returned the money to the bank on Thursday." He picked up his hat from the table and twirled it around in his hands. "She said she needed the money for a cash-only deal on a convection oven but changed her mind about buying it. The ring, she claims, belongs to her mother who had asked for it. The withdrawal and the timing seem odd to us. We'd like you to see if you can get her to open up about it—being her friend and all."

Liz stood up, feeling the hot flush in her cheeks. "I'm not going to spy on my friend, Stanley Houghton! Not for you or anyone! Naomi was working in her bakery that morning; she didn't kill anyone. She's not capable—"

"I'm not asking you to spy." He got to his feet and began walking to the door. "We want to clear her as a suspect too."

Liz felt a sinking in her stomach. *Naomi's alibi is sound, but she isn't out of the woods. Come to think of it, neither is anyone else.* "I don't think the withdrawal is unusual; she's always looking for ways to improve her business." She paused, knowing she was taking Houghton's comments personally and that the possibility of blackmail was most certainly in the chief's mind. As for the ring, was it possible that Moriah Mason had indeed asked Naomi to bring it to her? "This mysterious companion of O'Rourke's could answer a lot of questions," she said.

"Believe me, we're tracking down every lead." He rubbed a hand over his jaw. "Please report anything suspicious—and be careful." In spite of the kindness in his eyes and the softness in his tone, she wanted him to leave, and she wanted the lump in her throat to vanish with him.

Liz waited at the open door, hugging herself for warmth as the chief pulled on his boots and zipped up his coat. Seconds later he left, his feet kicking up a whorl of snow from the porch. She lingered there, watching him trudge toward his cruiser that was parked beside the inn.

As she stood pondering the chief's warning, she became aware of movement off to her left. Someone was shinnying down the big oak tree several yards from the inn's entrance. There was no mistaking Felix Horner in his buffalo plaid hunter's cap with the ridiculous flaps hanging down. Liz stared in amazement. *Being small has its advantages*, she thought, *but who knew Horner had such strength and agility?* Then again, it was likely a skill he had developed to assist him in drawing a bead on a particular species.

When the police cruiser turned a corner and disappeared down the street, Felix stepped away from the tree and strode up the walk, hands in his pockets, binoculars swaying on his chest.

It appeared that Felix was giving Chief Houghton the slip. Well, she supposed she couldn't blame him. He had been the one to discover the body and had spent considerable time answering questions. You couldn't blame him for trying to avoid answering more. She wasn't happy about the police hanging around either. Even though her guests seemed to be in good spirits, a murder nearby was not exactly a selling point for the inn.

She waited on the porch as Felix approached. He was such a funny little man with fussy habits. There was something about him that invited a good-natured taunt. "Well, you just missed him," she said.

"Who?" he asked innocently, mounting the steps in boots with thick trousers stuffed inside.

"Chief Houghton, of course." She smiled wryly, stepping backward into the inn and holding the door open for him. "I saw you by the big evergreen over there waiting for him to leave."

He laughed, showing his small, even teeth. "After enjoying the antics of a particularly delightful brown creeper, I didn't want to spoil the day with more infernal questions." He spread his fingers, which were encased in leather gloves. "Did you know, the creeper has a clever way of spiraling upward from the bottom of one tree trunk and then flying down to the bottom of another? He creeps slowly with his body flattened against the bark, probing with his beak for insects."

Liz groaned inwardly, expecting to be serenaded by yet another birdcall, but Felix picked up the subject of Houghton's visit instead.

"I've nothing against the good keepers of the peace, but they should be out finding Mr. O'Rourke's killer instead of bothering innocent folks minding their own business." He sniffed—rather like an offended dowager—and pulled out a handkerchief to clear his glasses that had instantly fogged up in the warm foyer. His eyes were like two watery glaciers.

Liz looked down. Those colorless orbs unnerved her, but she spoke casually. "The chief brought some interesting news. Apparently, Mr. O'Rourke had someone with him. The police think he may be the one who shot him."

Felix continued rubbing the thick lenses, peering through slitted eyes in concentration. "So the Mountie gets his man; I suppose we should congratulate him," he said jauntily.

"Well, not yet. They haven't caught him, but he does seem a very likely suspect since he hasn't shown up to inquire about his friend. You didn't see anyone with Mr. O'Rourke at any time, did you?"

"Why, no," he said, as pleasantly as if they were discussing the weather. "Never laid eyes on O'Rourke until he showed up in your parlor. Now, if you'll excuse me; I've gotten quite chilled out there in the wild. Besides, I want to try my hand at the creeper's portrait while it's fresh in my mind."

Liz returned to the inn's sitting room, happy to see that it was unoccupied. She curled up on the couch. Where had O'Rourke been before his arrival on Tuesday night when he fixed the furnace and charmed them all? Who was his mysterious companion? An ex-con like O'Rourke? The hardest question concerned Naomi. Had she really withdrawn cash for an oven and then changed her mind? Or was there some other reason? And Rachel. Did she know more than she had revealed?

We were going to meet in the woods across from the farm. But the police were there. Liz recalled the words blurted out in the bakery through a barrage of tears. That flash of red she had seen—was it Rachel's coat? Was it Rachel heading toward the woods to keep her tryst with O'Rourke. Poor Rachel—poor, deluded Rachel. Looking for love in all the wrong places. Or was she an extraordinarily good actress? Could she have killed him? Perhaps with the help of someone else—the mysterious companion?

But what had O'Rourke wanted from Naomi? Was he hoping to reconnect, to rekindle an old flame that she had extinguished? Or was it something else? She had been behaving strangely. Liz thought back to that day with the Material Girls when Naomi had mindlessly nibbled one cookie after another. And later she had nearly collided with Orpah Hausen's buggy upon returning from visiting her mother.

She leaned back against the couch and tried to relax. Houghton's news was good news. A prison inmate with a grudge against Shane O'Rourke, or whatever his name actually was, had traveled with him.

Had he come into Pleasant Creek and taken revenge on his former prison mate? That had to be it. There was nothing to worry about, because the police would find him. She could enjoy these days with her guests and get ready for a fun community event without concern for flashes of red in the forest or for the well-being of her friends.

Yet, as the fire crackled softly in the grate and a picture-perfect landscape stretched beyond the sitting room window, Liz felt a gnawing in her stomach that had nothing to do with hunger. Things just didn't add up.

11

Liz remained in the sitting room, too unsettled to move. How had life become so complicated? Her mother used to say, "'Tis the gift to be simple," drawing on the old Shaker song "Simple Gifts."

'Tis the gift to be simple, 'tis the gift to be free

'Tis the gift to come down where we ought to be,

And when we find ourselves in the place just right,

'Twill be in the valley of love and delight.

Life had certainly become complicated for her mother who had been raised in a simple Amish home. But realizing that the man she was about to marry was involved in fraud, she had left everything she loved to protect her family. She had had every right to feel sorry for herself, but she hadn't allowed bitterness to overcome her. She had begun a new life of purpose and meaning, and brought Liz into it.

Am I "in the place just right," having come full circle to Pleasant Creek where Mother was raised? She sighed. With an unsolved murder and a friend under suspicion, it wasn't exactly a "valley of love and delight" just now.

Liz jumped when the door burst open with a flash of crimson and yellow. Rachel Hausen burst in, blonde hair wild and disorderly, her face nearly as red as her coat, and tears streaming down her cheeks.

Behind her a bewildered Sarah stood, hands outstretched in hopeless apology. She quietly closed the door, leaving Liz alone to deal with the impetuous Rachel.

"Rachel! What's the matter?" Liz rushed to her and took hold of her arms, fearful that she might crumple to the floor. "Tell me—"

"Oh, Miss Eckardt!" Rachel wailed, "I don't know where else to go. I—"

"Hush," Liz said over the loud sobs. "Come and sit down. Tell me what's happened." She pulled her toward the couch by the fireplace, unmindful of the wet marks Rachel's high-heeled boots made on the carpet. She eased the girl's arms out of her coat. "Let me get you some hot tea."

"No, no!" She shook her mane of hair, but allowed herself to be nestled onto the couch.

Liz sat beside her, keeping a comforting hold on her arm. Did Rachel ever enter a room in a normal manner? After barging into Sweet Everything and flinging herself at Naomi, she had talked about the handsome man who'd turned her head. Liz had been able to settle her down before she went back home. So what was wrong now?

"I don't know what to do. I can't stay there, and I can't go back. I left everything because Shane said . . ." She broke off in a fresh outburst of weeping.

"Rachel, get hold of yourself and stop crying," Liz said firmly. Had her own mother felt like this when a man betrayed her? Though she felt desperately sorry for Rachel, she knew the girl needed some common-sense advice more than she needed tenderness. Though twenty-one, she was untested in the ways of the world, and O'Rourke had not been a good teacher. Now thrust back into a less-than-welcoming family fold she was still a lost sheep.

"I'm sorry," Rachel mumbled, colorless lips trembling. She wasn't wearing any makeup at all today—probably a wise concession considering the taboos of the Hausen household. Liz recalled the thick black mascara Rachel had worn that first day. Today a long denim skirt replaced the tight designer jeans. She sat up straighter, pulling a little away from Liz's supporting arm, and wiped her nose on the tissue Liz supplied. Finished, she wadded it up in hands clenched in her lap.

"You said you can't stay there. Do you mean at home with your mother and father?"

She nodded and took a shuddering breath. "Ja. I am to stay in the Grossdawdy Haus and keep away from Ben and Essie."

"Your brother and sister?" Liz asked.

Rachel dropped her eyes and sniffed again. "I can help Mutter with chores, and I don't mind the Grossdawdy Haus, but—" Swallowing hard, she finished with a whisper, "I miss them."

Liz waited, imagining the gawky twelve-year-old boy Sadie had told her about. And nine-year-old Essie—Esther, Sadie had said—described as a picture of her mother.

"Those two are kept so tight in the family nest, they may never learn how to fly," Sadie had said with a disapproving grimace. "Nearly nine years between Rachel and Ben, twelve for Essie who barely knows her big sister."

Liz felt a lump in her throat. Snug in a loving Amish family nest was nothing to disparage. She had great respect for their way of life and learned much from it, as had her mother. "It must be hard for your father," she said quietly to Rachel. "He's lost two sons . . . then when you left—" She took a sustaining breath. "Your parents want the best for you—and for your siblings. It may just take some time—that is, if you plan to stay in Pleasant Creek. You don't have to go back to Chicago, you know." She broke off, remembering how lost and alone she herself had felt at one time. "But if you do plan to go back . . . You said you had some family there. Couldn't you stay with them again?"

"We didn't part in a good way," Rachel said. "Aunt Chloe was good to me at first, and when I moved to an apartment she even helped me get my old car. It still works—most of the time. It's how I got here from Chicago." She lowered her eyes to her fidgeting hands. "But when I told her I was going away with Shane . . . well, I don't think she wants anything more to do with me."

Liz's mind alternated between compassion for Rachel and frustration over all the unanswered questions. *O'Rourke hadn't come to Pleasant Creek with Rachel. Instead he and a mysterious companion hitched a ride with a trucker. Why was that?*

"And besides, I don't have a job anymore. Shane told me—" Her lip trembled when she said his name. "He said I wouldn't need one, that we would go away together and start a new life. Now he's gone." She wagged her head sorrowfully. "After Vater kicked him out of the barn I never saw him again until somebody killed him—probably that Naomi Mason!" She stuck out her lip like a petulant child.

Liz gasped, completely ignoring Rachel's accusation about Naomi. "He stayed in your barn?" she asked incredulously.

"It was just that one night. He didn't have any place to go."

"But he checked in here at the Olde Mansion Inn," Liz interrupted.

"Yes, but he didn't have a reservation until the next day. Vater was away on a buying trip, and Mutter let him stay in the barn." She twisted the wadded tissue. "Mutter let me bring him some supper and blankets. We were just talking there in the quiet . . ." Her eyes took on the soft, undeniable glow of youthful love but were quickly shadowed with pain. "We didn't know he would come home early. We didn't hear the buggy, and suddenly there he was with his shotgun. I've never seen him so angry." She covered her face with her hands.

A shotgun? Liz was aghast, picturing Ephraim like a threatening prophet of doom descending on two hapless sinners. She knew many Amish men had shotguns and used them for hunting. But O'Rourke was killed by a handgun—a .38, the chief had said. Was it possible that Ephraim possessed such a weapon in addition to the shotgun? "Rachel, what did your father do?"

"He just stood there with that gun in his hand and told Shane to get out and never come near his house or barn again."

This was new information, which neither Ephraim nor Orpah had shared. Could Ephraim have killed O'Rourke, believing he had ruined his little girl? Had he been waiting in the woods that morning when the lovers were to meet? That would be completely against everything the Amish stood for. A murderous Amish man seemed impossible, but human passion could push even the best of men to do the worst of things. Liz thought of Simeon Graber, a respected Amish leader whose unscrupulous dealings had caused her mother to flee Pleasant Creek and the family she loved.

Rachel began to fidget more nervously. "I was going to meet Shane that morning," she whispered, "but I saw the police . . ."

"Where was your father?" Liz asked.

"I don't know."

"Do you think he would . . . hurt Mr. O'Rourke?"

She lifted frightened eyes. "No!" She shook her head in vigorous denial and repeated, "No, no! Vater would never . . ."

"Rachel, I'm just trying to get at the truth. Someone shot Mr. O'Rourke, and it wasn't Naomi. Do you know who the other man was that was traveling with him?"

She looked up at Liz with eyes as big as harvest moons. "I didn't know anyone came with him. I've never met any of his friends. We were going to be together—just me and him."

Either she is innocent or she is one terrific actress, Liz surmised. "The chief says the man had red hair and wore big sunglasses and a hat," she added. "Did Shane ever talk about someone like that? Ever mention someone in passing, or—"

"No. He didn't talk about his friends."

"He could have met him in prison," Liz went on. "The trucker picked out someone from the police files who may be the man. They're looking for him now. Rachel, are you sure?"

She put her hands over her ears and shook her head from side to side. "I don't know anything about any other man." She bit her lip. "Is he the one who killed him? Why would he do that?" she wailed. "We were going to be together—just Shane and me." The repeated words drifted off in a heartbroken sigh. "Oh, Miss Eckardt, what's going to happen to me now?" She began to cry again.

Beans lifted his head from the thick rug by the fireplace and trained his eyes on them. His small ears folded over like flags at half-mast, and a bewildered expression appeared on his short two-tone muzzle. Slowly he raised himself and padded over to the couch, stopping at Rachel's feet. He sniffed and nudged her, then sat back heavily on his haunches to stare at her.

"I think Beans likes you," Liz said, giving Rachel's arm a squeeze. "Don't you, big boy?" She reached down to pat the formidable head. When she'd first met the English bulldog, she had thought him completely useless and ugly to boot. What stroke of ill fate had decreed that the animal should be part and parcel of the inn? Now she looked into the watery brown depths of his soulful eyes and wondered what she would ever do without him. "He won't hurt you," she told Rachel, who had thankfully stopped crying.

"He has a funny name," Rachel said, giving the dog a tentative pat. Then she began to stroke his bristly fur with one delicate hand.

Beans scooted closer and let his big head drop on Rachel's boots. He made a soft, grunting noise, almost as if he were expressing sympathy for the poor girl.

"Yes, I think you've made a friend." Liz cleared her throat. "Now, Rachel, what would you say to staying here at the inn for a little while—just until you get things sorted out?"

What am I saying? Don't I have enough trouble without taking on a confused, bereaved girl who may even have committed murder? But it would give her some space, some time to think, and she'd be out from under the harsh eye of her father.

Rachel stared at Liz with wide gray eyes and seemed too stunned to speak.

"There's a small spare room on the second floor that I think will suit you," Liz continued. "The Holmes sisters are staying on that floor too. They'll be just a few doors down. You'll have to help out at the inn though. Sarah and Kiera can show you how to be useful. We're very busy around here, especially with the party and auction just around the corner."

"I—I never thought—" Rachel's eyes roved around the cheery sitting room with its soft chairs and colorful cushions, the bright pictures on the walls. "I always wanted to be a guest here." She frowned suddenly. "Are you sure it would be all right?"

"Of course it will be all right," Liz said. "I am the owner, after all. But you need to tell your mother where you'll be, and, if you haven't already done so, you need to phone your aunt. She may be very worried about you." She helped Rachel into her coat and walked with her to the door. Beans followed along behind, a hospitable grin on his face.

As Rachel started down the porch steps, Stefan was climbing up in his galoshes, arms laden with firewood. He wore his navy peacoat with his signature red ski cap—a sight that still gave Liz pause. He nodded first to Rachel and then to her. "Miss Elizabeth," he said, a wry smile on his weathered face. "I thought you might be low on fuel for this evening." He stepped out of his unlatched galoshes and passed through the door she held for him.

In the sitting room, he piled logs into the rack beside the fireplace, adding the final two to the dwindling fire. He stood, watching the wood catch, sparks igniting and flaring in a blaze of orange and yellow. He rubbed his gloved hands together and turned to Liz. "If this cold snap lasts much longer you'll be out of firewood. I hope your supplier has more I can pick up."

"I'll give him a call," Liz said absently. She was thinking about how to broach the subject of why he had lied about his whereabouts on the morning O'Rourke was shot. She studied his weathered face, the sea-blue eyes—sharp and searching like a mariner's eyes. Had he ever sailed the high seas?

He took off his cap, causing his shock of white hair to flare out. "No need to bother. You got enough to do. I'll call him—got my cell right here." He pulled off his gloves and reached into his coat pocket, then the one on the other side. "Must have left it in the shed," he said sheepishly.

She smiled. His tendency to forget his cell phone had become legendary. "No hurry. We're good for another day or so at least." When he began to head for the door, she said decisively, "Stefan, could we talk for a minute?" She gestured to one of the chairs. "Take off your coat. I'll get a couple of Sarah's excellent scones and be back in a sec." She hurried into the kitchen before he could object.

He was still on his feet when she returned with cinnamon raisin scones and two cups of steaming coffee. "Been working outside all day. Don't want to get your nice chairs dirty." He had smoothed his disarrayed hair and looked at her expectantly, a slight frown creasing his forehead.

"Nonsense. Sit. Make yourself comfortable." She handed him a small tray holding coffee, napkin, and scone. "Things have been so crazy around here, we've hardly had time to say two words to each other." She laughed, hoping to put him at his ease. She was about to ask some difficult questions, and she was anything but relaxed.

She waited until they had both polished off their scones. She took a sip of coffee, peering at him over the rim of the cup. "I've been meaning to ask how you're getting along," she began.

The frown deepened. "Right as rain, miss."

"There's been so much shoveling this season," she said. "It must take a great deal of stamina." She looked at him steadily, waited a few seconds, sensing his tension. "I heard that you've been visiting the clinic."

He dropped his eyes and set down his cup.

Liz hurried on. "One of the members of our quilting group is a nurse. She saw you there and wondered if you were all right."

"It's nothing," he said quietly. "Just the usual checkup business. You know, when you get to be my age . . . but I'm as strong as I ever was. I can still—"

"I know you were there last Wednesday morning," Liz said evenly. "What I don't understand is why you told Chief Houghton and me that you went home to get your sander and feed your dog. If you had said you were at the clinic, you would have been cleared as a suspect immediately."

Stefan's rough fingers trembled slightly as he set his cup down with great deliberation. After a few seconds of silence, he looked across at her. His shoulders drooped, as though something inside had crumpled. "You know that I've been happy working here," he began slowly. "After Nell's passing and retiring from Cross Furniture, I thought there was nothing for me—" He bit off the words and reached for his cup again before continuing. "Working here at the Olde Mansion Inn from time to time has been good for me—very good. I've made friends here, and you've been very kind." He broke off and looked down at his gnarled hands. "But I understand if you have to let me go."

Liz stared in consternation. "Let you go?" *Because he'd been out at Jaynes Lake? Because he'd shot Shane O'Rourke?*

"I didn't want you to know."

She felt her breath stop. "What didn't you want me to know, Stefan?"

"About the clinic. My heart isn't what it used to be, and the doctor says I should slow down." He stared again at his large hands clamped over his knees. "I didn't want you to know because I was afraid I'd have to leave here; that you'd want someone younger and stronger." He looked up at her with moist eyes.

Overcome with relief, Liz stared at him. When she could pull herself together, she reached across the expanse between them and covered his work-worn hands with hers. "Stefan, you've been such a help to us this season at the Olde Mansion Inn. I couldn't have asked for a harder worker, and we've all become very fond of you." She looked into his anxious eyes, feeling her heart melt. She'd had no idea how much this seasonal job meant to him. "There's no shame in having to slow down a little. There's a lot you can do here at the inn, and we can get someone to help with the heavier work when needed. Is that okay with you?"

Stefan rose, his ruddy face glowing. "It's more than okay, and I'm sorry for not being completely honest. It's just that I worried . . ." He fumbled with his hat and then with a decisive gesture plopped it onto his head. "I guess I'd better get back to my work," he said throatily. "Thank you, Miss Elizabeth."

12

"You don't have to go with me, Liz. I know you're pretty busy right now," Naomi said as Liz climbed into Naomi's Hyundai.

Naomi's voice over the phone had been dull and anxious when Liz had called earlier to offer to go with her to visit her mother at Serenity Arms. Naomi needed the support of her friends.

"I'm never too busy for you," Liz said. "I brought some of Mary Ann's homemade jelly candies. You said they were your mother's favorite."

"That's very thoughtful of you," Naomi said, snapping her seat belt in place over her tan cashmere wrap coat. "I hope Mother appreciates them. She has her good days when she remembers things and seems very happy. Then there are days when everything's a blur—well, everything except Willie John." She gave Liz an apologetic smile. "I hope this will be one of her good days."

Willie John, Liz recalled, was Naomi's half-brother, the war hero who was feted every Memorial Day in the Masons' little hometown in Maine. The dead son who absorbed his mother's life and memory.

"After Willie John's father died, Mother remarried," Naomi continued softly. "My father, Connor Mason, was good to all of us and very generous." Naomi looked down at her hands. "I miss him so much!"

Liz touched her friend's arm, remembering how hard Naomi had taken her father's death. It hadn't been very long ago, and now she was embroiled in all this mess. *Poor Naomi. Life could deal some pretty powerful blows sometimes,* she thought sadly.

Naomi sighed and continued. "My father was wealthy and became powerful in the state of Maine, so when Willie John died in Desert Storm, he made sure the town made a really big deal of it for my mother's sake. I was still in high school at the time. It was as though all the trouble Willie John got into before entering the military never happened. Mother always believed he was a hero—misunderstood in his youth but a hero in the end."

No wonder Naomi wanted to get far away from home and the accolades for the brother she had never really known, Liz thought. Had Naomi ever received her mother's undivided attention or affection? As they drove toward Serenity Arms, she hurt for her friend who was under such great strain.

"I've been a real dud lately," Naomi said, as though intuiting Liz's empathy, "but I'm glad you came with me today." After a few seconds of silence, a small smile played over her pale features. "And I promise not to run into any buggies today."

A hint of the old Naomi, Liz thought. She glanced at the pink angora scarf and tam that gave her friend's complexion a tinge of color. Naomi's eyes revealed the tension she had been under since the investigation began. "These past few days have been something else," Liz said, cinching her seat belt as Naomi started the car. "But the roads are clear and the sun is shining today." She gave Naomi a bright smile. "I always feel better when the sun is shining. Why is that?"

Naomi shivered and turned up the heat. "It's still awfully cold, isn't it?"

"It sure is," Liz said, wishing she could hug away Naomi's hurt.

Naomi kept her eyes trained on the road. She slowed to give space to an Amish buggy ahead of them signaling to make a left turn. When the road cleared, Naomi said, "At least we're not driving one of those. Then we'd be really cold." She sighed softly. "The Amish are a hardy lot. You've got to admire that."

When Naomi grew quiet again, Liz was pretty sure her friend was thinking about Rachel, the girl who had unleashed her anguish on the one she blamed for her boyfriend's death. It must have been very hard for Naomi to hear. "Rachel had to blame someone," Liz said quietly. "In a way, Rachel was as much a victim of a handsome face and a fickle heart as you were. But there's no way she can deny the kind of person he actually was. The police have confirmed his illegal activities, aliases, and prison sentences."

After a long silence, Naomi asked in a hushed voice, "Do you think she did it?"

Liz let her breath out in a slow stream. "She was jealous enough, I think, but it's hard to imagine that she would kill the man she still claims to love. And even if she did, she's hardly strong enough to pull a dead body up an incline." She stopped as the images replayed in her mind.

"The police seem to think I'm strong enough," Naomi said bitterly. "Just call me Amazon woman!" She turned sharply around the next corner. "Well, I didn't shoot him."

"I believe you—and the police have a new lead," Liz said brightly. "Chief Houghton came by yesterday to tell me that he talked to a truck driver who picked Trevor up on Highway 30 and brought him to Pleasant Creek."

Naomi groaned. "I thought I saw a police cruiser parked by the inn again. Maybe they should be paying rent." A mirthless grin touched her lips before quickly fading.

Liz let a few seconds elapse before saying, "He said there was another man with him."

Naomi turned to look at Liz. "With the chief? Or with Trevor?" The Hyundai wobbled slightly and stabilized when she returned her eyes to the road.

"With Trevor," Liz clarified. "The trucker said the man didn't talk, just slumped down in the seat with a hat pulled low over messy red hair. The truck driver couldn't describe the stranger beyond that, but there was no mistaking Trevor Winston."

"Guess misery loves company," Naomi said morosely after a few seconds.

"The truck driver said he brought them to town on Monday, but Mr. O'Rourke—that is, Trevor—didn't show up at the inn until Tuesday evening. The police are trying to find out what he did and where he went during the hours before checking in at the Olde Mansion Inn. All I've learned is that he spent Monday night in the Hausens' barn."

"Maybe this friend who was with him can shed some light on that," Naomi said as she pulled into the spacious parking area in front of Serenity Arms and turned off the engine.

"If and when they find him," Liz said. She got out of the car and walked around to join Naomi, hooking her arm through hers. "He seems to have disappeared, but the truth will come out. It always does."

Naomi seemed to stiffen; then she moved rapidly to the door of the facility, her dark hair swinging over the shoulders of her coat. "I just want it all to be over," she said under her breath.

When they entered the room after a soft knock on the door, Moriah Mason leaned forward in her chintz-covered chair. Elegant in a mauve pantsuit with a tailored white blouse, she looked rather like a diplomat ready to give orders to a private secretary. A closer glance into the pale blue eyes showed a fragile, unsure woman, her snowy-white hair curved around her face in a modern cut—courtesy, no doubt, of the in-house beauty parlor.

"Hello, Mother," Naomi said, leaning down to kiss her cheek—a cheek remarkably smooth for a woman her age. "You remember my friend Liz."

The pale eyes focused on Liz but retained their dreamy quality. "Hello, dear," she said.

"I brought you something, Mrs. Mason," Liz said, unwrapping the box of jellied candies and pressing it toward her.

"That's very kind," she said and with a heavily veined hand took the box and laid it in her lap.

"Have one, Mother," Naomi encouraged, sitting down on the small settee and unbuttoning her coat. "They're the ones our friend Mary Ann makes, your favorites." She patted the cushion next to her, inviting Liz to sit while still engaging her mother in conversation. "You said you liked the lemon ones best, didn't you?"

"Very nice," she said, looking down at her lap. "Very kind." She picked the box up but set it down on the oval table next to her chair without taking a piece. She looked at each of them in turn, eyes restive, as though trying to remember something she wanted to say.

Now Liz pondered the elderly Moriah—a handsome woman by anyone's measure—who actually looked a lot like Naomi. She had the same narrow-bridged nose, high cheekbones, and pink-toned skin. Both women were tall with trim figures. Only their eyes presented a marked contrast. Moriah's were a very light blue while Naomi's were a chocolate brown, like her father's, no doubt.

"Can I get you something, Mother?" Naomi asked after they had been sitting together for about fifteen minutes, Liz and Naomi chatting to each other while Moriah Mason sat dully in her chair. Naomi reached across to touch her mother's arm, her dark eyes melancholy and filled with filial devotion. Whether the affection was returned or not, Naomi loved her mother with a fierce passion. "Would you like some juice or ginger ale?"

Moriah Mason didn't answer but continued to stare into the portrait of her son on the table beside her chair. Her brow furrowed as though she was concentrating or trying to remember something. Presently, she turned to her daughter, her eyes luminous. She looked eagerly into her daughter's face. "I had the nicest visit from a young man today."

"Oh?" Naomi said pleasantly.

Liz sought the pale eyes that had become suddenly animated. Was she speaking in real time or harking back to some memory?

"He knew all about my William," Mrs. Mason went on. "He was with him in the war, and we had the nicest time talking about him. How brave he was, what a good soldier and . . ." She paused, her face glowing. "He's very anxious to see you. He said to tell you he would be back."

"Who was he?" Naomi asked hesitantly, the lines in her forehead deepening.

"He—he didn't give his name," Moriah said. She put her fingers to her temples as though to pull out the information hidden inside. "I remember now. He said he was the new chaplain here—replacing Reverend Peters."

"What was his name, Mother?"

The dreamy smile remained. "He said he would be back again and wanted me to tell you that." She began rocking in her chair, eyebrows knit in thought. "But what was his name?" She clasped and unclasped her hands. "Why, dear, I don't think he told me."

Naomi stood, her dark eyes troubled, her voice calm. "I'm glad you had a nice visit, Mother. I'll check with the office. I'm sure they will know his name so that I can thank him. But Liz and I have to go now." She patted her mother's hand gently and kissed her cheek.

When they had closed the door to Moriah's room, Naomi turned to Liz. "I need to have a word with the director," she said. "I'll just be a minute; I'll meet you at the door."

Liz waited, taking in the ambience of a foyer designed to mimic that of a gracious home with comfortable sofas and chairs, shining end tables bedecked with fresh flowers, and gilt-framed paintings on tastefully decorated walls. Elegant lamps glowed even in the light of the afternoon. *Would that every mother could spend her golden years in such luxury.*

Moments later, she saw Naomi turn into the hallway and come toward her. Her face registered confusion and weariness, but she said only, "Let's go" and led the way back to the Hyundai. She started the engine but stared through the windshield without putting the car in gear. "No visitors signed in to see my mother today except you and me." She exhaled wearily. "And there is no new chaplain. Reverend Peters is still the only chaplain here. I'm afraid my mother is growing more and more delusional."

Liz didn't know what to say. Moriah Mason had seemed lucent, even more energetic than the last time she was there. "She seemed so . . . sure . . . so happy." It was easy to believe she'd really had a visitor who talked to her about her son. "I'm sorry, Naomi."

Naomi sighed and guided the car out of the parking lot. They drove without speaking for a while. Then Naomi said pensively, "She's never done that before. You know, made someone up. And it seems odd that Mother thought the visitor knew about Willie John and that he would want to see me."

Liz recalled the words. *He's coming back; he said to tell you that.* "Strange," she said. "Maybe she made up the visitor because she wanted you to hear of her son's bravery from someone else. So you would love him as she does. But you know your mother better than I do . . ." She let the words fall away.

"Oh, Liz," Naomi said with a deep sigh. "When did life become so complicated? Wouldn't it be nice to just take off—maybe to Hawaii or somewhere warm—and just forget everything?"

"Only if I get to go too." Liz hastened to underscore Naomi's vision of happier days. "Hawaii would be perfect. We could go surfing on Maui and drink out of coconuts while we bask in the sun. I don't know how to do the hula—or surf—but I bet we could learn."

"I wish that dude behind me would learn how to drive," Naomi said with irritation. "He could have gone around. I gave him plenty of room but he's sitting on my tail."

Liz turned around and saw that there was indeed a vehicle close behind the Hyundai. A black motorcycle roared along with the sun bouncing blindingly off its silvery chrome. Motorcycles were rare around Pleasant Creek in the cold month of February. Sadie had an old pink Harley that she liked to show off, but it was securely parked in her barn until May. The big black bike behind them bore down closer. "I wonder if he's lost or missed the main highway," she said.

"He's not going to find it on my bumper," Naomi fumed.

Suddenly the motorcycle pulled out and swerved around from the left. The cyclist, dressed in black jacket and chaps, zoomed close to the Hyundai, the visor of his black helmet totally obscuring his face and hair. He was a frightening apparition curved over a menacing black machine.

Liz felt her heart pound. "What in the world?"

And then he began to cut back in front of them. They were going to hit him! The trendy slogan raced across her mind: *Start seeing motorcycles.* They were going to see this one up close and personal. "Naomi, watch out! We're going to—"

In a flash, the biker whipped around them as Naomi pumped the brakes. The motorcycle wobbled crazily, missing them by inches. Then the biker gunned his motor and veered off onto a dirt road, his wheels kicking up a rooster tail of dust as he sped away.

Naomi turned onto the shoulder, bringing the car to a shuddering stop. Her hands were white as chalk where she clutched the steering wheel. She turned an ashen face to Liz. "Are you all right?"

"I think so. You okay?"

Naomi leaned back hard against the headrest. "Am I to be a target for every vehicle on the road? First an Amish buggy, now this. What is wrong with people today anyway?"

It could have been a teenager thirsting for speed, Liz supposed. Or some nut getting his jollies out of frightening two women alone on a country road. If only she could have gotten a license number or knew enough about motorcycles to describe this one. "Have you ever seen it before?"

Naomi wrapped her arms over her coat. Her eyes were shut, her lips a colorless line. "I haven't seen a motorcycle around here in months. It can't be more than thirty degrees outside. Who rides a bike in the middle of winter?"

"No one in their right mind," Liz agreed. "We've got to report this." She scrounged on the floor for her purse, which had been thrown off the seat when they stopped suddenly.

"Report what?" Naomi said. "That we saw a nut on a bike? We have no license number. No name."

"Has anything like this happened before? I mean since —" Liz broke off. There had been a lot of talk about Naomi and her involvement with the murdered O'Rourke. Was some "good citizen" trying to scare her, to warn her that she'd better come clean? It seemed ridiculous. No, it *was* ridiculous. Liz thumped her purse down on the seat between them. "I'm definitely going to report this to the chief, but right now we need a cup of coffee. Want me to drive?"

Naomi shook her head. "I'll be fine, but if it's all the same to you, I just want to go home. I don't want to talk to the police anymore. There's nothing they can do about a crazy guy showing off on his motorcycle."

"But we shouldn't just ignore this. No one has the right to—"

"Please, Liz." Naomi gripped the steering wheel and leaned forward to rest her head on it. "Look, I would love to have a cup of coffee and a good long chat. I've missed that and—" She looked across at Liz with pleading in her eyes. "There are things I want to tell you . . . but not now."

Liz felt her pulse speed up. "How about tomorrow?"

"Not tomorrow," Naomi said. "Candice has the day off—and Jenny can't help with the day's baking, so I'll be up to my ears."

"I could come over and help."

"No. Liz, you have enough on your hands without babysitting me. We'll talk soon," she repeated. "I promise."

13

"I think we may finally be out of the deep freeze," Sadie proclaimed as she and Liz headed out to Sew Welcome's van. With breakfast over and guests' needs tended to, they were off to Cross Furniture to pick up the display racks Jackson had graciously donated for the community quilt auction.

"Look at that fabulous sun!" Liz exulted. "It's sure to melt some of this ice and snow. Now if these balmy temps will just hold for Friday." She opened the passenger door of the colorful old van.

"We'll hold a good thought," Sadie said, pressing the engine into noisy action. She was wearing twill pants—a step up from jeans, a casual coat of brushed suede, and low-heeled boots. Her short white hair was brushed back in a no-nonsense style that framed a face shining with extraordinary good health. "By the way, how's young Rachel working out?" she asked.

Liz raised an eyebrow and expelled a slow breath. "Well, she's been surprising me, I must say. She didn't bat an eye when I asked her to give the sitting room a thorough going over, including the fireplace—under Sarah's supervision, of course. She even helped with breakfast this morning."

"Rachel was trained to do her share and more of the housework," Sadie said thoughtfully. "But I wonder if you're not biting off more than you can chew having her around. We still don't know if she was involved in that poor man's death. Rachel was always a devious child."

"It's hard to believe she was involved," Liz responded pensively. "She seems to have been really in love with the guy." She folded her hands in her lap. "Sadie, is there anything more you can tell me about Rachel's father?"

Sadie gave Liz a quick glance before returning her focus to the road. "You have a reason for asking?"

"Well, you know the police discovered that O'Rourke—or Winston—was in town at least a day or more before arriving at the Olde Mansion Inn. Turns out Rachel snuck her boyfriend into their barn on Monday night while Ephraim was away on a buying trip. Orpah said it would be all right for him to sleep there because it was such a cold night and he didn't seem to have any place to go. She even supplied him with blankets and food."

"That would be Orpah's way. She wouldn't allow man or beast to suffer."

"But Ephraim came back unexpectedly and found Rachel and O'Rourke in his barn. They were just talking, according to Rachel, but apparently Ephraim flew into a rage and ordered the man off his property." She paused while Sadie took this in.

"So you think maybe he was bent on punishing the man who was taking advantage of his little girl?" Sadie asked. "Ephraim comes across as bitter and something of a tyrant, but to actually kill . . . I just don't think so. It would be against everything the Amish believe." She paused. "Still, a few have been known to fall from grace." Sadie turned onto the street where Jackson's furniture company was located. "Have you heard any more about the mystery man who hitched a ride with the victim?"

"No, but Chief Houghton says they're tracking a number of leads. They think he was a fellow inmate when O'Rourke was in prison. When they find him, all this speculation about the murderer will probably be explained and things can get back to normal."

Normal for Naomi too? How her good friend fit into all of this

Liz couldn't fathom, but something just wasn't right. Liz shook her head, eager to dispel her dismal thoughts as they drew up to the long two-tone brick building that housed both the factory and sales floor of Cross Furniture Company.

"Isn't it wonderful of him to make the quilt racks for us? He's such a community builder—and not just because he's looking out for his image as mayor. He truly cares." Liz heard the exuberance in her voice and attempted to temper her enthusiasm. "He was glad to help once he knew why we needed the racks."

A smile played at Sadie's lips. "You mean he was eager to help once he knew *you* were the one needing them." She swung the van into an open slot near the loading dock with expert finesse.

Liz made a dissenting noise but felt her cheeks warm. Just because she had taken extra care with her hair and makeup and had chosen the petal-pink sweater she knew he liked didn't mean she was trying to attract his attention. Just because she was hoping he'd be at the furniture store and not away on some mayoral mission . . .

"Well, I think it's high time the two of you stopped pussyfooting around and got serious!"

"We're not pussyfooting," Liz said fervently. "We're just friends getting to know each other." She whipped her purse onto her shoulder in preparation to get out of the van. Sadie could be as colorful as the Patchwork Bomb. "Just park this thing and let's get those ladder racks loaded," she said with a mock glare.

"Certainly," Sadie responded sweetly, her grin widening. "And I hope you can wait while I check out a few items. I'm in the market for a couple of bedside tables."

At the counter, Mae Westerfeldt greeted them warmly. She was a middle-aged woman with sleek black hair threaded with silver. The brown eyes behind red-framed glasses lit with recognition. She'd been the head sales clerk, receptionist, and go-to person at the company since Liz had come to Pleasant Creek, and Liz knew Jackson prized her grace and professionalism.

Mae picked up a phone and quickly punched a button. "Jackson asked to be notified when you arrived," she said, holding a manicured hand over the mouthpiece. "You can go on back."

Liz and Sadie found Jackson in the entryway between the factory and sales floor giving instructions to two workers who were polishing the rounded rungs of a quilt rack stained in a beautiful golden pecan finish.

Liz felt the quick intake of her breath as Jackson smiled a greeting and waved them forward with his muscular arm. Dressed in white shirt and tan pants, he might have come directly from a business meeting—or perhaps he was on his way to one. Little grass grew under those brown leather oxfords. She found herself more than a little pleased that he was in today.

"We've got the racks ready for you—hand-finished and polished—complete with nonslip pads and double brass hooks on the sides." His mellow voice echoed in the foyer. "We built them to your specifications. Hope they fill the bill for the auction."

"They're perfect," Liz breathed. "It's really wonderful of you." She hoped she was making sense; it was difficult to think straight sometimes when faced with those glowing hazel eyes and rugged features.

"All for a good cause," he said. "I'll have the guys load them for you."

"We're on the east side—not far from the loading area," Sadie said helpfully.

"I think they'll recognize the van," Jackson said, giving Sadie a slight bow. "It's one of a kind, that's for sure."

"Don't get smart," Sadie said with feigned irritation.

Jackson held out his palms in a gesture of conciliation. "What?" He turned to Liz. "Did I say anything?"

Liz went for a look of bewilderment.

"Just to show there are no hard feelings, how about a cup of coffee?" Jackson said. "Mae just bought one of those fancy coffee machines for my office. I think it knows how to answer the telephone and do data entry too."

"Not for me," Sadie said briskly. "I'm going to see if your tables are as good as you say they are." She waved Liz off as she turned to go into the showroom. "You go ahead. I'll meet you in a few once I've finished my shopping."

"After you, Liz," Jackson said when Sadie departed. When they reached his office he stepped in and pulled out a chair for her. "Everything all right at the Olde Mansion Inn?" he asked as he took a seat behind his desk. "You've certainly had your share of excitement."

"More than I ever bargained for," she said dismally. "But with the police searching for the man your driver picked up with O'Rourke, we might all be able to relax."

"Hmm." Jackson drummed his fingers lightly on his desk—a sign that he was thinking and perhaps troubled. "A guy who's a million miles away from here if he's got half a brain." He looked at her with penetrating eyes, their usual radiance darkened. He cleared his throat and got up swiftly. "Coffee—that's what I promised. I think it might be just what you need. Come on over here and help me with these pods. Mae ordered enough flavors to confound anyone."

She joined him at the credenza where the rack of little cups was lined up next to the brew machine. He ran his finger across the cups, mumbling the names printed on the lids, "Mocha Crème Delight, Chicory Roast, Smooth Colombian Blend . . . Who writes this stuff?"

"That last one sounds nice. I'll take that." Liz reached for it. When she accidentally brushed his hand, she felt a flush rise to her cheeks.

He took the little cup gently from her fingers. "Let me do it for you. I need the practice." He placed a mug under the dispenser, pressed a few buttons, and the machine began to whir and hiss. He turned around and leaned against the credenza next to her, close enough that she could smell the rich outdoorsy aroma of his aftershave lotion. She grew even more flustered when he suddenly grasped her hand. "Liz, you look tired. Are you sure you're all right?"

She shrugged, warming to his concern and trying her best not to make too much of it. They were just friends. She gently withdrew her hand, aware of the lingering effect of its warm pressure. "We'll all be relieved when they catch up with that mysterious companion of O'Rourke's. Naomi especially . . . but thank you for your concern."

Jackson made a second mug for himself and they carried their coffees back to their chairs by his desk and were quiet for a long moment. "Jackson," Liz began, "do you know anyone who rides a motorcycle around here?"

"Motorcycle?" His brow furrowed deeply at the unexpected question. "Well, I've seen a few—not lately though. There's been too much snow." He paused. "Has someone on a bike been bothering you?"

"Not exactly." She described her experience with Naomi on the road back from Serenity Arms. Recalling the black-helmeted invader on his intimidating machine, she felt a chill creep up her spine.

"Did you report it? Give a description to the police?"

She shrugged. "I tried to convince Naomi that we should, but she begged me not to. She's had about all the questioning from the police she can stand. Besides, she thought it was just some kid trying to scare her. We couldn't see his face at all, and there was nothing unusual about the motorcycle—except that it was black and silver and scary-looking."

He was quiet for several seconds, then said, "Claude Payne's boy lives out that way. He has a bike—likes to get a rise out of folks when he roars through the neighborhood. And that kid who lives with Granny Hanover is quite a biker too."

Liz drew a breath and let it out slowly. "It was pretty unnerving, I have to tell you. But Naomi just wanted to go straight home without talking to the police. There's been a lot of talk about her involvement with the victim. A lot of whispering behind her back. I'm afraid she feels like a social pariah."

"All the same, Chief Houghton should know. There are lots of loose ends about this crime. You never know what might be important." He leaned forward in his chair and looked at her intently. "The fact that an unidentified murderer is still at large . . . Well, you have to be very careful. Don't trust anyone." He frowned. "That birder who found the body—is he behaving himself?"

"Felix Horner?" She shrugged. "I know you don't like him, but he's really quite harmless."

"Liz, it has nothing to do with liking or not liking. I just find it odd that nobody knows anything about him. He's so far under the radar that he might not exist at all—at least by the name of Felix Horner."

She stared at him. He'd been checking up on the guests at the inn. He wasn't leaving it to the police. She decided to lighten the conversation. "Why, Jackson Cross, are you worried about me?" she asked coyly.

His serious expression told her he wasn't amused. "Of course I am." He thrummed his fingers on the desk again—more vigorously this time. After a moment he added, "That's what friends do. They look out for each other." He narrowed his eyes. "I know you. I know your trusting nature. You give everyone the benefit of the doubt. I bet you took in stray animals when you were a kid."

She shrugged, secretly pleased. "Guess it's my Amish roots."

He wagged his head. "Is that why Rachel Hausen is staying with you instead of with her folks?"

"Only because her father doesn't want her around. Says she's a bad influence on the two younger children in the home. Besides, she was distraught. She had no place to go." Agitated, she stood and took a few steps away from her chair, then paced back again toward Jackson. "She can't go back to Chicago. She quit her job, believing her handsome prince would take care of her. She was duped, Jackson, just like what happened to my mother." She stopped. She hadn't intended to mention her family. And why was that lump thickening in her throat?

Jackson, who had risen when she did, shortened the distance between them. "I know you want to help her. I get that. It's just that . . . well, you can't blame me for being concerned about you." He put his hands gently on her shoulders. "I just want you to be careful." He tilted her chin up with his right hand, the warmth of his left still burning through her. "And I just want to help."

Liz swallowed against tears that threatened to well up. Why did he have to be so all-fired sweet to her? She took a step back, not trusting herself to speak right away. "I know," she said with a sigh. "Thanks. And thank you for the coffee—and again for the quilt racks. They'll be perfect for the auction. We've made plans for the whole day—great food, music, dancing . . ." She gulped, thinking how nice it would be to float across the floor in Jackson's arms. *Don't go there*, she chided herself.

"I think it's a great project," he said. "Folks can enjoy the day and at the same time help refurbish the children's wing of the hospital." He took the empty cup she handed him. "I'll be there, and I hope you'll save a dance for me."

As Liz stepped out of the office door, she saw Sadie coming toward her. She hoped the glow she was feeling wasn't visible on her face and that her feet were really touching the floor.

14

"I brought it down to show you, Liz." Violet Holmes said excitedly. She held a ruffled lavender dress still on its hanger against her ample chest. "I got it in a delightful little boutique in town and simply couldn't resist." She made a small pirouette and grinned, causing her dimple to show.

Vera sat across from Liz in the dining room, finishing her coffee with a sardonic expression, her back rigid against the chair. A hopeful sun beamed through the window. Rachel and Sarah had cleared away the dishes and could be heard chatting in the kitchen. Everyone, it seemed, had slept in that morning, Liz included. Everyone except Felix, who, according to Sarah, had come down for his morning oatmeal and then headed out in search of a tufted titmouse to complete his collection of chickadee portraits.

"What do you think, Liz?" Violet asked, twirling around once more. "I thought I'd wear it to the Valentine's Day party." She leaned down to whisper in Liz's ear. "I think Stefan's going to ask me for a dance."

"I think you'll be stunning," Liz said, trying to stifle a chuckle. Violet had such a disarmingly childlike aura it was impossible not to be charmed by her. *Stefan and the Lady of the Purple. Now if only Vera will keep her domineering nose out of her sister's budding love life.*

"Really, Sister, you must begin acting your age," Vera said. Even on rare occasions when Vera smiled, there was no hint of a dimple. "That filmy thing would be more appropriate for a teenage hop."

Violet was not to be swayed by her sister's remark. Her eyes continued to sparkle, and she even gave Liz a secretive wink. She pulled the dress away from her body to admire it and smiled with appreciation. Tilting her head to one side, she pursed her lips as though a thought had just occurred to her. "You know? You may be right."

"Of course I'm right. How much did you waste on that piece of fluff?"

Intent on some distant thought, Violet appeared not to hear her sister. She touched the ruffled neckline. "The last time I had the chance to wear a dress like this one," Violet said, her blue eyes taking on a dreamy quality, "Aunt Annabelle was making dresses for us that summer. Remember, Sister? Even though she'd been sick and was still weak she wanted to make dresses for us. We were invited to a party, and we'd only brought play clothes."

Annabelle. The night they arrived at the Olde Mansion Inn, didn't the sisters speak about visiting their aunt and Felix in the Midwest—miles away from their East Coast home? Liz glanced at Vera, whose eyes narrowed disapprovingly. Liz thought she heard a muffled harrumph escape the stern lips. Vera didn't much like her cousin, but then Vera didn't much like a lot of people.

"She stitched it by hand as she lay propped up on pillows," Violet continued. "Oh, it was a beautiful dress—a little paler purple than this one. I couldn't wait to wear it." She sighed suddenly and dropped down on a chair. "But it was ruined—completely ruined! Grape juice, wasn't it, Sister? A terrible accident."

"It was no accident!" Vera broke in. "Felix did it on purpose. I saw him with the glass in his grubby little hands."

"Oh, he was just a little boy, Sister." Violet protested.

"Just a little *brat*," Vera corrected. "You know he couldn't stand his mother paying attention to anyone but him. Remember how he'd steal the cookies that were intended for all of us and threw the flowers you picked for her down the well?"

"Maybe, but we've quite forgiven him, haven't we, Sister? See what a polite and smart man he's become. Let bygones be bygones, I always say." She tossed her soft crop of curls and laughed. "No accidents this time. I'm going to wear this dress to the party, and it will be such fun! Sister, what are you going to wear?"

"I haven't given it a thought," Vera said, sniffing. "I shall be quite busy helping Sadie with the auction. You know she depends on my business expertise."

Business expertise? Sadie needs Vera's business expertise? Liz struggled to keep from rolling her eyes.

Vera suddenly pushed back from the table. "Enough of this nonsense." She shook her finger at Violet and gave her head a little jerk in the direction of the window. "And you had better watch yourself with that old man out there. He's probably out to snare someone to cook his meals for him and wash the dirty socks he throws under the bed." With a huff, she left the room and headed for the stairs.

Now Liz did give way to laughing. She reached across the table to touch Violet's arm. "You're going to look beautiful in that dress," she said firmly. "And Stefan is a perfect gentleman. You can be sure of that. Just don't pay any attention to that sister of yours this morning. I think she got up on the wrong side of the bed, don't you?"

Liz's heart warmed at the sound of Violet's sweet laughter. She was a woman who had learned the secret of aging gracefully. She enjoyed life and looked for the best in everyone. And she could do a whole lot worse than cooking and washing for Stefan.

She watched Violet sweep up the dress in her arms and make her way out of the dining area. *A woman with her outlook on life could do a lot for Stefan*, she thought. He'd been alone so long. She thought about her handyman's confessed fear of losing his job—of becoming too old to be of use to anyone. Whatever time he had left, she hoped he would know that he had a place in life—and maybe in someone's heart.

Beans, who had been sleeping in a patch of sunlight, made a contented sound deep in his throat. He raised his head and yawned luxuriously.

"Doesn't worry you, does it, boy?" she said, looking into his drooping brown eyes. His left ear wiggled as though he'd heard and completely understood. Then he dropped his big head back down onto his paws.

Liz smiled and leaned back on the chair with its comfy padded seat and let the sun warm her face. What would *she* wear on Friday? She realized she hadn't given any thought to that until now. Maybe her red sheath with the chiffon drape—in honor of Valentine's Day. It wasn't new, but it was comfortable and made her feel fabulous. *And Jackson will be there.* She allowed herself to savor the concern in his perceptive eyes, his gentle urging for her to be careful. *Listen to yourself*, she chided. *The day is about raising money for the children's hospital and* you're *thinking about that dance Jackson asked you to save.*

At the unusual sound of knocking on the front door, she dismissed her reverie. "I'll get it," she said to Sarah, who poked her head into the room. "By the way, did I thank you and Rachel for getting breakfast for everyone today?" she called over her shoulder. "I don't know when I last had the luxury of sleeping in." She opened the door.

"Mrs. Hausen!" Liz said with surprise.

The diminutive woman in black Kapp and cape stood on the threshold, her heart-shaped face pallid in the morning light. Her buggy stood at the curb, and a sleek black horse stamped idly on the pavement. "I am sorry to disturb you," Orpah Hausen said nervously, shifting a large canvas bag. "I have brought some of Rachel's things . . ." She broke off as though not knowing how to proceed.

"Of course, Mrs. Hausen. Won't you come in? Please," she added at the woman's hesitance. "I'll get Rachel."

"Is she—?" Orpah's dove-gray eyes widened with some unnamed fear.

"She's just fine. Here, let me take that for you." Relieving her of the canvas bag, Liz clasped Orpah's arm and urged her inside. "I know she'll be glad to see you."

"Only for a moment. I must get back."

Liz stiffened. *Back to her severe, unyielding husband who had asked his own daughter to leave his house?*

As though Orpah had divined Liz's thoughts, she said in a small voice. "Ephraim is only doing what he thinks is right." She gnawed her lower lip. "He—really does care about Rachel. He just—" Orpah left the words hanging and stared down at her reddened hands.

How hard it must be for her, Liz thought. She smiled. "Wait here. I'll be right back."

She hurried to the kitchen where Rachel was busily filling salt and pepper shakers. Everyone had vacated the main floor; mother and daughter could talk in private in the cozy sitting room. What she wouldn't give to have such an opportunity with her own mother. In a moment, she returned with Rachel in tow.

"Mutter!" Surprise lit Rachel's face. She approached her mother hesitantly at first, then flung herself forward to hug her.

"Rachel, why don't you take your mother into the sitting room?" Liz said. "I'll ask Sarah to bring coffee and some of those cinnamon rolls she made this morning. I need to check the guest rooms for clean towels. Since you and Sarah did all the work to prepare breakfast, that's the least I can do." She moved off as she spoke, gesturing for the two women to make their way to the sitting room.

In a significant departure from his usual indolent behavior, Beans lumbered behind her, the soft pads of his feet quiet on the stairs.

With fresh towels from the third-floor hall closet, Liz opened the door to the Sunrise Room where Felix was staying. The single-occupancy accommodation boasted a blend of contemporary and antique furnishings. Aptly named, its east-facing window afforded a magnificent panorama of the morning sky. Felix had made no mention of it. Did he appreciate the breathtaking sunrises others had remarked upon? Perhaps he couldn't see the sky for the birds. She smiled at her fractured take on the old saying.

The walls, painted in eggshell white, contrasted well with colorful art and cushions, placed just as she'd left them. The coverlet on the double bed was drawn up neatly to the pillow line and folded over. No clothes or personal items littered the room, and suitcases were closed and stored on the antique luggage rack. To each piece, a small lock was attached. *Unusual*, she thought vaguely. But then, Felix was a fastidious person.

A check of the bathroom revealed the same tidiness—used towels loosely folded and placed on the walnut-finished vanity, personal items zipped up in a small leather bag. She placed clean towels on the racks and went back into the Sunrise Room.

She'd been in here many times, attending to every detail for the comfort of guests, but now she felt suddenly as though she were a voyeur about to be discovered. Recent comments echoed in her mind. Vera had called Felix Horner a brat as a child and said he had deliberately ruined Violet's dress because he was jealous of his mother's attention. Were these the bitter ramblings of a crotchety old woman? Had Felix become the "smart, polite man" Violet thought he was? Both sisters said they hadn't seen or heard from their cousin in years. Strange that he would suddenly show up and want to join them at the Olde Mansion Inn.

Jackson had been cool toward the man from the beginning. A study in contrasts, those two—Jackson's rugged masculinity and Horner's somewhat affected, delicate manner. Jackson had insisted that whether he liked Horner or not had nothing to do with his caution. "I find it odd that nobody knows anything about him," he had said as they sat sipping their coffee in his office. "He's so far under the radar that he might not exist at all."

Apparently, Jackson had not left the investigation to the police. He had counseled her to be vigilant, that you never knew what might be important. *There are so many loose ends about this case . . .*

Chief Houghton had confirmed Horner's employment as a groundskeeper of a small Chicago park. And he was related to the twins. But beyond that not much was known about him. Jackson was right. She stood in the middle of the room feeling oddly uncomfortable. Perhaps some mild snooping was justified.

She surveyed the desk that took up a large portion of the south wall. Dusting it was part of the usual housekeeping routine, but it was covered with books and papers—the only cluttered space in the room. An artist's portfolio lay in the center, along with a three-tiered box of colored pencils and a rough sketch of a bird on a snow-covered branch.

She moved closer, studied the drawing. Nothing spectacular, but the lines were good, the bird recognizable. The titles of the books angled on the corner of the desk had predictable titles: *Birds of North America. Nature's Songbirds.*

She spied a pencil that must have rolled onto the floor and bent to pick it up. As she did so, she saw that something was caught between the desk and the wall. A rolled-up paper of some sort. She put her hip against the desk and gave it a little shove to release the fallen object, which dropped to the floor. It was a long scroll. She picked it up with every intention of simply placing it back on the desk. Instead, curiosity aroused, she began to unroll it.

It was a blueprint, soiled and creased and unlike any building design she'd ever seen. It showed a kind of walled garden with abundant trees. There were small sheds and large plots measured off with cage-like crosshatching. Not a farm. An aviary possibly? Given Horner's fascination with birds, it wouldn't be surprising that he might build his own private sanctuary for them.

Put it back, she told herself. *The man's private papers are his own.* But she found herself scanning the neat hand-printed writing. At the top center were the words "Annabelle's Aviary." An eleven-year-old date was etched in the left-hand corner and in the right, the somewhat blurred architect's identification. "Ellerton, Inc., of Chicago."

Annabelle's Aviary. His mother's name was Annabelle. She remembered that Horner had mentioned it in an aside when he told everyone at breakfast about his trip to a bird sanctuary. "Quite a serviceable collection of birds and habitat," he had said importantly. "Nothing as grand as my Annabelle Aviary would . . ." And he had stopped abruptly as though he'd been caught thinking out loud. Liz recalled the surprising coldness that briefly washed over his eyes.

Not as grand as his aviary *would have been*? Was that what he'd started to say? Had he planned the aviary in his mother's honor? But she had died a long time ago when the Holmes sisters were young women. It was sad to think of Felix Horner carrying around the blueprint for years. His dream—what might have been. An aviary dedicated to his mother. Why had he not carried out his plans and built it? Or had he?

A low growl outside the partly open door startled her—not so much because Beans almost never growled but because suddenly Felix Horner stepped into the room. Liz dropped the blueprint, which quickly coiled up and rested accusingly at her feet.

"I came to bring some fresh towels," Liz began, feeling a rush of blood to her face. "And to give your room a quick airing . . ."

Felix stood still as a statue on small booted feet, arms at his sides as though at attention. A camera bag hung over the shoulder of his wool jacket. He had removed his cap, and his pink scalp shone through thinning strands of hair. His nose was red from the cold as he removed his steamy spectacles, revealing colorless, glittery eyes. He glared at her, then at the scroll at her feet.

Liz was aware of Beans standing rigidly behind Felix and panting quietly. He had stopped growling. If he had been trying to warn her, it was too little too late! Now, what was she to say for herself?

"I—saw that something had fallen behind the desk," she began, willing her heart to stop banging in her chest. *What's the big deal anyway?* It was standard practice to tidy the guests' rooms every day. She was only doing what she could to ensure his comfort. But the man standing just inside the door of the Sunrise Room was clearly not pleased with her ministrations. She stooped to retrieve the blueprint and laid it carefully on the desk.

Horner's voice cut like shrapnel. "Your police department has already thoroughly searched this room; I did not expect my privacy to be further invaded by the hotel management."

"Please understand, Mr. Horner. I had no intention of invading your privacy," she said firmly. Then more quietly she said, "Is there anything I can get for you?"

"Certainly not," the little man said, his lips barely moving. Was he gritting his teeth? Presently he added, "Mind you, I appreciate the amenities of this establishment . . ." He lifted his glasses, peered at the smudged lenses, then replaced them on his nose with a quick jerk of his left hand. The action worked oddly like magic. The anger in his face disappeared, leaving a flat, pallid oval. His rigid stance relaxed; his whole bearing seemed to change. "That is to say," he amended with a small smile, "Thank you for your courtesies." He stood aside for her to leave.

She scooped up the pile of used towels from the end of the bed and whisked past without another look at him. "Come along, Beans," she said and lifted her chin to walk down the stairs as sedately as she could manage.

15

The next morning Liz woke to the sound of dripping eaves. A quick check of the weather channel advised of a warming trend. The mercury would climb to a balmy forty-five degrees. She dressed in corduroy slacks and a merino jersey sweater in bold black and white stripes, and topped it off with a red infinity scarf. Nothing like bright clothes to give a girl confidence.

The night before she'd been surprised by a call from Jackson just before the ten o'clock news. "There's a new diner up at the north end of town. The mayor ought to pay his respects. Think you could join me for a late lunch—maybe around two?"

She'd been stunned into silence. Then he had added, "I thought we might swing by the Hanover place—maybe get a look at the motorcycle Tim rides. Might pass the Payne place too."

He clearly wasn't leaving her report of the motorcycle incident to chance—or to Naomi, who was reluctant to tell the police. She had felt herself smiling into the phone as she accepted his invitation. Most likely, he knew she wouldn't refuse since lunch included a little sleuthing. As she arranged the folds of her scarf, she wondered about the approach-avoidance game that both of them seemed to be playing. They were clearly drawn to each other, yet unwilling to—what? Give up their independence? Risk making a mistake?

She hummed as she prepared Eggs Benedict Strata—an online recipe that included generous amounts of lemon juice and took only a short time to prepare. She would have the usual oatmeal and wheat toast available for Vera, who seldom strayed from her usual breakfast. With any luck, Liz thought, she'd avoid Felix who was probably already engaged in his early morning routine of bird-watching.

She opened the back entrance for Sarah, whom she had instructed to sleep in today. She and her husband, Isaac, had hosted a special dinner for their church gathering the night before. Sarah always worked very hard, and she deserved a little time to rest. "How did your dinner go?"

Sarah hung her cape on a peg by the back door and secured her apron over her blue cotton dress. Her light complexion glowed with good health; her blonde hair shone beneath the little black Kapp that showed off her fair coloring more distinctly than the white one she'd worn before her wedding. "It went very well, and my Isaac was such a help. Mutter says he may well be an angel in disguise." She grinned and took a quick breath. "Now, what can I do?"

"The strata is ready. See if you can find the silver trivet for the long baking dish. Rachel is seeing to the coffee and tea service." Liz grabbed her oven mitts. "By the way," she said, reaching for the casserole, "is everything all right with you and Rachel? I know it was quite a surprise to have her suddenly underfoot."

"Ja," Sarah said thoughtfully. She pulled the silver trivet from a low cabinet and placed it on the counter. "But with Kiera taking time off to study for her tests, Rachel has been quite helpful. I never knew her very well when we were growing up. She was—"

Sarah struggled for the right words. *The words to say that Rachel was a bit on the wild side and likely not a companion Sarah's parents would approve of?*

"She was—well—different," Sarah finished with a sigh. "But she really is very nice. I think I like her."

Liz smiled, touched as she always was by Sarah's simple honesty. "I'm glad she's been helpful. She really needs a friend. She's been hurt by the man she thought loved her. It may take some time for her to trust again." She placed the casserole on the trivet and followed Sarah into the dining area.

They went through together into the dining room where Violet and Vera sat nursing cups of coffee. Just outside the dining area, Felix hovered over his cell phone, talking inaudibly. Liz wasn't sure why the sight surprised her. He was a park custodian, a single man on a bird-watching vacation, not a harried businessman tied to his phone. What business could he possibly be discussing? Nothing pleasant to judge by his tight jaw and rapid shaking of his head. Instinctively she pitied the person on the other end of the line and braced herself for a dressing down today after being summarily dismissed from the Sunrise Room the day before.

Finishing his call, he pocketed his phone and tripped jauntily to the table. "A delightful morning, ladies!" he chirped. "Our feathered friends have been unusually talkative today. I believe they know spring is on its way." He took a chair to the right of Vera, who not-so-subtly edged closer to her sister on the left.

"I should say so," Violet agreed heartily. The full sleeves of her purple paisley blouse flared out as she held her cup toward Rachel for a refill. "It's so nice to see the snow and ice melting, though I think this part of the country is quite suited to snow, don't you, Sister? I do love the way it sparkles in the sunshine."

"I say it's about time we had some decent weather," intoned the redoubtable Vera, who made no reply to her cousin and scrutinized Rachel over the top of her spectacles. While Violet had warmed to the troubled young Rachel, Vera's disdain for her was thinly disguised.

"Eggs Benedict Strata," Liz announced, placing the savory casserole on the table. "I think you'll enjoy the lemony hollandaise sauce that adds just the right touch to the eggs—and the English muffin crumbles are fresh from the bakery."

———————— ///////////////////////// ————————

The morning passed quickly with the usual chores to tend to, which included bookkeeping that Liz had let slide with all the excitement of the week.

Promptly at two, Jackson appeared wearing khaki slacks and a cable-knit sweater beneath the brown leather jacket that was his favorite. Though he always looked sharp in his mayoral dress coat and tie, she liked the casual attire, which lent an aura of youthfulness and daring.

It wasn't that Jackson didn't possess those qualities—and more—but he took his responsibilities very seriously and sometimes needed to be reminded about all work and no play. But Jackson, who crafted fine furniture and looked out for the interests of Pleasant Creek's citizens with equal passion, could never be called a dull boy.

"Afternoon, Liz," he greeted her cheerily, glancing around the foyer and up the staircase. "All quiet on the home front?"

"I'll just get my coat," she told him, aware of the way he took in her bold—and, she hoped, attractive—outfit. "I'm anxious to sample the new restaurant—Italian, isn't it?"

"I believe it's called Pasta Heaven. Guess we'll see how heavenly it is."

The weatherman had indeed smiled on them, for the day was bright and warm enough to send water cascading down drainpipes and gutters. They rode companionably, their conversation centering around the forthcoming community event and the renovation of the children's hospital. Pasta Heaven's bold red and green sign was impossible to miss as they turned onto North Columbia Street. It was settled in the middle of a block of boutiques and specialty shops with ample diagonal parking.

They chose entrées from a variety of dishes with such names as "Divine Bruschetta," "Cherubic Tortano," and "Blissful Lasagna." "Eternal Breadsticks" were served, along with olive oil for dipping. In spite of the rather corny monikers, the food was excellent, including the "Angelic Tiramisu" they ordered for dessert.

"I really enjoyed that," Liz said when lunch ended and they were once again in Jackson's comfortable sedan.

"It was all right, wasn't it?" he agreed. "Pasta Heaven may prove to be a good asset to our fair city." He turned off Columbia and headed toward the outskirts of Pleasant Creek.

Liz knew they were headed to the Hanover farm, which she and Naomi had passed on the way to Serenity Arms. "How do you plan to get a look at his motorcycle?" she asked. Jackson usually had a way of getting around a problem—sometimes in very ingenious ways, but mostly by simple friendliness, letting folks know they were important to the community.

He shrugged. "Granny Hanover doesn't get many visitors; she's always glad to see me," he said, a humorous glint in his eye. "That's their place just beyond Gruber's barn."

Years earlier, fire had destroyed Carson Gruber's home and crops along with several outbuildings. The barn, charred and badly damaged, stood like a sad specter over the land, a testament to the fate of the once-prosperous family. No one had wanted to build on the property, and some claimed the barn was haunted. "That place always gives me the creeps," Liz said.

"It's a real eyesore, but it's so far out of the way and shrouded from the road, nobody much cares," Jackson said, frowning. "Something should be done, though. An empty building can draw an unhealthy clientele."

A few minutes later, they pulled up to the Hanover place. Jackson parked between the house and the freestanding garage. "I'll go up to the door. You take a look inside the garage. If the cycle is there, see if it matches the one you saw. Tim should still be at work. His shift doesn't end until five."

"Won't Mrs. Hanover view that as rather intrusive?" she asked.

"Granny can't see more than five feet in front of her. Besides, I parked this way so you wouldn't be visible from the front door."

Liz watched him stroll easily up the walk and press the bell. After a full three minutes, it became obvious that either Mrs. Hanover wasn't home or she wasn't going to answer the door. *So much for worrying about being invasive.* She stepped out, walked around the rear of the car and stood on tiptoe to peer into the narrow windows in the garage door.

The garage was an unkempt conglomeration of tires and engine parts, oily tools, and assorted junk. At the far left was a motorcycle with a block of wood under the rear wheel to keep it from rolling. A helmet lay on a cluttered worktable nearby.

"What do you think?" Jackson said, returning to stand beside her.

"Couldn't have been him," she said with a mix of relief and regret. "The cycle that nearly ran us off the road was all black and silver—and huge." She shivered, remembering how the machine had advanced toward them, drawing closer and closer. "This one is red and a lot smaller."

"Guess Tim's off the hook," Jackson said, taking her elbow. "You all right?"

That was something about Jackson—he could read her mood. He could sense how the sight of the motorcycle had unnerved her. She nodded. "I just wish I knew why he came at us like that—whoever he was."

"Naomi has no idea?" Jackson asked, rubbing a hand over his jaw as they walked back to the car.

"No, but people have been talking about her connection to the man who was killed. It's even been affecting her business. I just hate to see that happening. Naomi has worked so hard to build up her bakery and to establish herself in Pleasant Creek."

"I know," he said quietly. "I'm sorry." He put an arm loosely about her shoulders. "I checked on motorcycle registrations. If the DMV's records are up to date, there's one more in Pleasant Creek—that is, besides Sadie's pink Harley. I'm thinking we can rule her out. It's Simon Payne, and he could have been driving along the route that leads from Serenity Arms to town center. Shall we make one more house call?"

She nodded, warming to his strong touch. Inside and out he was a man you could depend on, and right now, she could easily have pressed herself into his arms. Bold stripes and bright flags of color aside, she felt vulnerable and in need of comfort. Still, she pulled away and climbed back into the car.

An elderly man responded to their ring at the Payne family's yellowing farmhouse. A widower and long retired, he appeared groggy and somewhat disoriented, as though he'd just awakened from a nap. "Ain't here," he said to Jackson's request to see Simon. "'Spect he's at the plant this time of day."

Jackson smiled, tentatively withdrawing the extended hand the man had made no move to shake. "Of course," he said pleasantly. "Hope you'll forgive the intrusion. You doing all right, Claude?"

Claude maneuvered his jaw in a clockwise motion as though he might be chewing tobacco with his toothless gums. He peered from Jackson to Liz and gave a shrug of his thin shoulders. "Tolerable," he said and repeated the word. "Tolerable."

"Did Simon ride his motorcycle to work today?" Jackson asked.

"Ain't been riding her anywhere. Durn thing's been in the shop all winter." He shrugged again. "Simon ain't had the cash to pay for the repairs. Good riddance, I say. Blasted thing scares what few chickens I got left." He pushed out his flabby lips and repeated the chewing motion. "You got a reason for asking, Mayor?"

"No, no. Just curious," Jackson said lightly. He extended a friendly hand once more, but the old man had already begun to shuffle away from the door. Jackson made a small deferential bow. "We won't bother you anymore. Good day to you."

"Not exactly the chatty type," Liz said when they were once again in the car and heading home.

"You should see him on one of his bad days," Jackson said, grinning. He sobered then. "So, we can eliminate our local boys. Well, at least these two. I can check into surrounding counties, but it would be a long shot. Your nasty motorist could have been anyone coming through town."

"It was probably just what Naomi thought it was—some kid speeding on a country road and showing off for a couple of hapless women," Liz said. "Sorry to waste your time."

"From my point of view it wasn't a waste at all." He gave her a sidelong glance before turning onto the county road leading to the main artery. "We had a good Italian lunch and . . ." He paused. "And I got to spend some time with a particularly attractive innkeeper."

Liz felt her cheeks grow warm. She made an appreciative noise but wasn't sure what she said in the glow of the moment. She leaned back in her seat with a sigh. Riding with him on a beautiful sunlit afternoon had been exhilarating, but all too soon it would end.

"Hey, isn't that your bird-watcher in that old Explorer up ahead?" Jackson said, his voice rising.

Liz craned her neck. "Uh . . . could be. Looks like him, and the car looks like the one he registered." She squinted to see into the car's rear window. It was Felix, but he wasn't alone. The man in the passenger seat wore a sportsman's jacket and dark glasses. A black ponytail was threaded through a hole in his baseball cap.

"Know who his friend is?" Jackson asked.

The Explorer turned off and sped away before she could get a closer look. "No one I know or have seen before," Liz said. "But there are plenty of folks around that neither of us knows." The police had described O'Rourke's traveling companion as a man with shaggy red hair, sunglasses, and a stained cowboy hat. The man riding with Felix had a black ponytail. And half the world wore sunglasses. Besides, Felix had every right to travel the road with whomever he chose.

Though Felix's companion didn't match the description of the man the police were looking for, it would be a good idea to have a word with Chief Houghton. *Every detail could be important*, Jackson had said, and she knew he was right. She thought about telling Jackson about the blueprint and Beans's foiled warning, but he probably wouldn't find the story funny. It would only add to his dislike of the funny little man.

"I still don't trust the guy," Jackson grumbled. "I think he's two eggs short of a full nest."

Liz couldn't help laughing—and it pleased her that Jackson was defending her from imagined danger. "Somehow I don't think he'd approve of that metaphor," she said, slapping his forearm playfully.

"I suppose I've kept you away from the inn long enough," he said with resignation.

"Almost long enough. I've developed a powerful thirst

suddenly—probably something in that heavenly pasta. Could we stop at the junction for a cola?"

Jackson brightened. "Your wish is my command."

With darkness gathering, Liz was back at the inn an hour later. Felix's Explorer was again parked in the lot. She went to her quarters to change, humming softly to herself. They hadn't learned anything about the mystery cyclist or who had killed Shane O'Rourke, alias Trevor Winston, alias who-knew-what, but she had thoroughly enjoyed Jackson's company. It had been an altogether lovely day.

She donned a pair of warm lounging slacks and an oversized sweater of green angora. It was to be a casual evening. She would have the fire going, and later, there would be a poetry reading by the local librarian.

Liz lingered at the window of her private sitting room, watching as dusk began to fall over the landscape. The huge oak that Felix had shinnied down stood tall, most of its leaves still clinging to branches that would hold them captive until spring shoots freed them. The wiry little man had been invading her thoughts frequently since the morning he'd caught her with his blueprint.

Ellerton, Inc. She'd not only made a note of it, she'd checked it out online and confirmed that the company was still in business. She pulled her cell phone from her purse and dialed Sadie's home number. "I need to make a quick trip into Chicago tomorrow. I'd like some company. You up for a six a.m. start, so I can be back by dinnertime?"

"You need more party supplies? Can't you get them here?" Sadie was clearly suspicious.

"Nothing like that. But it's important and it has to do with the—um—case."

"I'll be ready—with bells on," Sadie said.

Liz smiled and pocketed her phone. Then she stood, amazed at herself and what she had just decided to do.

16

Emily Bergdorf, guest lecturer for the Pleasant Creek Library Club, held a slim, tattered volume in her dainty hand. A white muslin dress covered her slight frame, and her black hair, parted in the middle, was drawn back in a bun at the nape of her willowy neck. *"Because I could not stop for Death,"* she read with rich accents, *"He kindly stopped for me - The Carriage held but just Ourselves - And Immortality."*

Liz smiled from her vantage point at the rear of the sitting room. Miss Bergdorf not only carried the first name of Emily; she possessed Miss Dickinson's petite, refined bearing as well. The Material Girls were hosting the reading for Liz's guests and a few local friends, all of whom seemed captivated by the lady and the verse.

Stefan sat next to Violet, his shoulder brushing her purple-clad one. From time to time, she cast admiring glances his way. Though he kept his eyes fixed on the speaker, a telltale reddening of his cheeks revealed his pleasure or perhaps his mild embarrassment. Liz felt herself smiling at their blossoming friendship. Was love sweeter once you've traveled farther down life's winding path?

On Violet's left, Vera sat with her hands folded stiffly in her lap, but her sharp gaze pierced the poet look-alike. Caitlyn was clearly enraptured, and Mary Ann's soft features glowed as the words spilled into the cozy room.

"We slowly drove - He knew no haste And I had put away My labor and my leisure too, For His Civility."

Liz felt a little chill pass through her. Of all the Amherst lady's poems, why had this one been chosen? Or was it mere coincidence, in light of the murder, that had everyone at the Olde Mansion Inn uneasy? A great deal of Victorian poetry focused on death, a daily fact of life. Still, the choice unnerved Liz as she cast her glance around the sitting room. Most of those gathered were women. She looked around for Felix Horner, but he was not among the rapt listeners.

She imagined him up in the Sunrise Room, bent over a sketch of some exotic bird, or studying the dog-eared blueprint of Annabelle's Aviary. She shivered, recalling the look on the little man's face when he'd caught her with the building plans. He was clearly angry—unreasonably angry. It was just an old drawing of a bird sanctuary, which she had picked up from the floor after it had fallen. Or was there more to it? Was there something sinister about that blueprint?

You're getting paranoid, Liz Eckardt, she told herself. But she knew with a little pang of guilt that she would be glad when the man packed up his portfolio and cameras, and left Pleasant Creek. *Beans would likely be more content as well.* She looked fondly toward the fireplace where the dog lay in his bed, a dreamy smile on his fat, friendly face.

The mild-mannered bulldog was considered as much a part of the Olde Mansion Inn as the gables in its roof, and he was generally accepted by everyone. Well, almost everyone. She couldn't help but smile at the memory of the gentle beast's low growl just before Felix had appeared in the doorway and caught her with the blueprint. The feeling appeared to be mutual.

I wasn't snooping, she told herself. *Not really. Oh, all right. I was snooping.*

Miss Bergdorf's slightly nasal diction continued in the sitting room. Liz glanced toward the door as she had done several times since the poetry reading began. Naomi had agreed not only to come for the event but to provide the refreshments as well. She'd been such a hermit of late, and it cheered Liz that Naomi might be getting back to her normal engaging self. She tiptoed over to Sadie and leaned down close to her ear. "Have you heard from Naomi?"

Sadie raised both eyebrows and shook her head.

Could Naomi have forgotten? Or changed her mind about coming? Certainly she had a lot to occupy her thoughts these days, but it wasn't like her to let the group down.

The lecturer continued with a biographical sketch of the famous poet: "After she studied at the Amherst Academy for seven years in her youth, Emily Dickinson spent a short time at Mount Holyoke Female Seminary before returning to her family's house in Amherst. Thought of as an eccentric by the locals, she became known for her white clothing and her reluctance to greet guests or, later in life, to even leave her room. Most of her friendships were therefore carried out by correspondence."

After another glance at the door, Liz retreated into the kitchen. Perhaps Naomi had come in the back way since she had refreshments to arrange on the cut-glass trays Liz had placed on the counter. But there was no sign of her. Sarah had left for the day as soon as cookie hour was over, leaving Kiera to prepare the coffee and tea for those attending the poetry reading.

"I'm not really interested in lectures," she had said earlier, claiming she got enough of those in school. But there was Kiera, standing just inside the door, green eyes alert with interest.

"When it comes, the Landscape listens - Shadows – hold their

breath -." Emily Bergdorf read. *"When it goes, 'tis like the Distance On the look of Death."*

"Any sign of Naomi?" she whispered in Kiera's ear.

"Haven't seen her. Haven't seen anybody in there," she replied and inclined her head to take in more of the grim lines of Dickinson's verse.

Liz smiled and left the kitchen door ajar for Kiera's benefit. She moved further into the kitchen, dialing Naomi's cell number. Five rings, six, and then Naomi's cultured voice said: "Thanks for calling Sweet Everything. Leave me a number and I'll get back to you quicker than you can say 'chocolate eclair.'"

But Naomi didn't call back, and Liz had an uneasy feeling. "Tell Sadie I'm going to run next door and be back as soon as I can," she told Kiera. "Ask her to go on without me. And see what you can pull together in case Naomi doesn't get here." With a worried sigh, she headed toward her quarters for her coat and purse.

The bakery was closed, the only light coming from the overhead electric sign that read "Welcome to Sweet Everything Bakery." It was round like a birthday cake with small red lights around the perimeter—like decorator roses. Liz recalled how they had pored over designs to select just the right sign that would attract shoppers. She had caught Naomi's enthusiasm and had been as delighted as Naomi when the sales began rolling in. She was a natural in business and creative too. No one could decorate a cake like Naomi.

Liz sighed. They had clicked from the beginning like two peas in a pod—or twin candles on a birthday cake. Each had bounced back from a disappointing love relationship, and each had decided to launch out into unknown territory and establish businesses in Pleasant Creek. Neither of them were Amish but each held profound respect for the tradition.

Though it seemed obvious that no one was inside Sweet Everything, Liz rattled the door just to be sure. She waited, peering into the darkness and listening for any sound of life. The rattling of the door seemed unnaturally loud in the quiet street with its smattering of snow left in small indented spaces along the curb. Naomi had likely finished early and gone home, perhaps had some supper and planned to drive over to the inn for the poetry reading.

Liz got into her car and drove toward the area of town where Naomi had built a small but elegant home with lots of greenery around it: stately elms, cultured arborvitae, with a carefully tended garden and lawn. Naomi's Tudor-style house was the last on the block and bordered at the back by Henneman's Woods. They had often walked together in those woods before coming back to Naomi's for cider and doughnuts or tall glasses of lemonade in summer.

She missed those companionable walks, those times of easy conversation. Would it ever be the same between them after the cloud had dissipated—when the truth of O'Rourke's killer was exposed and Naomi was no longer the focus of attention? The police were still looking for the man who'd been seen with the victim—a former cellmate of his. He couldn't possibly have anything to do with Naomi. Yet there was something too secretive about Naomi these days. Something wasn't right, and it nagged at her like an ache that wouldn't go away.

She turned onto Naomi's street. Though it wasn't quite eight o'clock, no cars moved, and houses appeared shuttered and dark. Naomi had mentioned that residents were demanding more street lamps for the relatively new community. It was even darker at the end of the street where the woods bordered Naomi's house.

As she turned into the driveway, her headlights flashed on a figure in the distance near the wooded area. She quickly backed up to train her lights in the figure's direction, but whoever it was leaped up and ran into the cover of pines. She had an impression of hunched shoulders and a hooded parka. The hood flew back, revealing someone with a long ponytail.

Stunned, Liz bolted from the car and ran around toward the woods. But whoever had been there was long gone. Was it a girl sneaking out to meet a lover? The figure had moved with a strong, swift gait but little grace. Could it be a man? She'd seen more than one macho guy with long hair drawn back. Her mind raced to the stranger she and Jackson had glimpsed in Felix's car. A stranger with long hair threaded through a baseball cap.

Naomi! Had something happened to Naomi? She ran back to the house, raced up the short steps, and rang her friend's doorbell. There were other houses close by, but what if whoever had run off into the woods had come for Naomi? She leaned on the doorbell, continuing to rap hard on the door. "Naomi! It's me, Liz!" Her voice echoed oddly in the quiet street.

Silence. She banged harder. A neighbor's dog began to bark. She thought she saw a faint light coming from the back of the house. After a few seconds that seemed like hours, the curtain at the side window moved. Naomi's head appeared in the glass, her brown eyes wide with confusion or fear or some emotion Liz couldn't read.

"It's me—Liz! Let me in!"

What's taking her so long? Several seconds passed before the door was finally opened to reveal a seemingly unruffled Naomi dressed in a paisley kimono, her rich brown hair loose about her shoulders. She stood in the doorway, quite unhurt, a woman spending a quiet evening at home. Only her eyes, wide and restive, gave any hint of trouble.

Relief mingled with frustration as Liz stared at her friend. "Are you all right? I thought . . ." She stopped the flow of words. Whatever—or whoever—she had seen, it might have had nothing at all to do with Naomi. "I was so worried!" she blurted out.

A sudden dawning spread over Naomi's face. "Oh no!" she said and brought her hands up to cover her mouth. "The poetry reading! I forgot!"

Forgot? She forgot? "Are you all right?" Liz asked again, stepping in and shutting the door behind her.

"I'm fine—only I'm completely embarrassed. I don't know where my mind is these days." She reached up to brush back a lock of chestnut hair. "I meant to take some of those chocolate eclairs from the shop to bring to your place—but I left without them. And I didn't think about the reading until just now. I'm so sorry, Liz!"

"But you didn't answer your phone," Liz protested. "And just now . . ." *Just now I saw a stranger lurking near your house.* She almost spoke these thoughts aloud, but why stress Naomi with imagined threats? Her mind raced as she stared at her friend. "I've been calling."

"I'm sorry." She paused and looked down. "Answering the phone hasn't been much fun these days. I've been ignoring it. I'm afraid I didn't look to see who was calling." Naomi had told her of crank calls. How could people be so heartless and unthinking?

Liz slumped down in the re-covered Edwardian chair that Naomi kept in the foyer. She didn't know what to say. Still reeling from worry, she took in Naomi's deeply shadowed eyes and pallid complexion.

The investigation had dragged on, demanding its toll and adding to Naomi's ever-present concerns for her mother.

Naomi shifted her weight as though she couldn't think of what to say—or as though she was poised to flee from Liz's scrutiny. She drew in a quick breath and let it out. "You can pick up something from the supermarket to serve at the poetry reading, can't you? Is there still time? I'll give you the money." She crossed her arms over her kimono. "I really am sorry."

"Don't worry about it, Naomi. Emily Bergdorf was just getting started when I left, and I told Kiera to scrounge up something from the kitchen. When you didn't arrive or answer your phone, I decided to pop over."

"Thanks, Liz," Naomi said, shaking her head as though to emphasize her gratitude. She fidgeted with her nails, which were blunt and uneven—very unlike her. She took a step toward the door. "I appreciate your concern for me, but I'm sure you have to be getting back."

An uncomfortable pause passed between them. Liz got the distinct impression that Naomi didn't want her to stay. Liz swallowed against the hurt of it; they'd always been able to talk. "If you need anything . . ." Liz let the sentence lapse and got up from the chair, drawing her purse strap over her shoulder. "If there's anything I can do, you'll call me, right?" She felt herself frowning as she fixed Naomi with her eyes.

"I will," she promised, moving closer to the door. "And once again, I'm sorry." She hung her head this time. "I let you all down—"

Liz stopped the apology by throwing her arms around Naomi. "This will be over soon," she said gently. "They'll find the answer; it's going to be okay." She gave Naomi a reassuring smile. "Now, I'd better get back before Miss Emily runs out of poems."

As she walked away, she heard the dead bolt click and saw the lights switch off. So much for the hermit coming out of hiding.

17

"She forgot?" Sadie asked incredulously as she snapped her seat belt over her lap. "That's not like our Naomi."

"No," Liz said thoughtfully. "But she hasn't been herself lately, and I guess we can't blame her." She started the engine of her Acura and drove away from Sadie's farm. It was six a.m., the next day after the poetry reading. Sadie was never late. She was wearing an azure pantsuit that brought out the blue of her eyes. Those eyes now flashed with irritation and confusion.

"She's been under so much stress with everyone talking about her and thinking she was responsible for Shane O'Rourke's death," Liz went on. "If that weren't enough, she worries about her mother, whose Alzheimer's continues to progress. The other day she rambled on about an interim chaplain who said he knew her son—the one who died during Desert Storm. She says this man came to see her and told her about her son's bravery."

"Poor Moriah," Sadie muttered. "She seldom talks about anything else but that boy."

"When Naomi checked with administration, she discovered there was no interim chaplain, that Reverend Peters was still on call there. No one had been to visit Mrs. Mason that day but us." Liz drew in a breath. The visitor had asked Moriah to assure Naomi that he'd be back. The exchange had bothered Liz, and she could tell that Naomi had been uncomfortable too. What if there really had been someone in the woman's room? What if saying he would be back was really a threat of some kind?

Sadie broke into Liz's thoughts. "Alzheimer's can be devastating. My aunt Hilda was convinced that Maurice Chevalier shared her supper every night." She eased out of her suit jacket and tossed it into the backseat, adding, "But Naomi's dealt with that for a long time and still managed to get things done."

They were quiet for a while as they whizzed along the highway. Sadie was good company, her heart solid gold, but she could raise difficult questions. When a person said they would do something, Sadie expected them to keep their promise, regardless of the sacrifice involved.

"She apologized over and over," Liz said at last. "She wanted to give me money to pick up something at the store, but I had already asked Kiera to see what she could find in the kitchen. Did everything go all right after I left?"

"Oh yes," Sadie said. "There were plenty of cinnamon scones and chocolate chip cookies. And believe me, by the time Emily finished her presentation we were all ready for refreshment. That woman does get into her subject. It was eerie to see her dressed in white with that black hair parted in the middle like a proper Victorian lady. Could give you the willies."

It did give me the willies, Liz thought, remembering the carriage of Death stopping to pick up his prey. She sighed. "Emily's good. You could almost believe the poet of Amherst had been resurrected."

She fell silent then, thinking about Naomi and about the figure she'd seen near her friend's house. Had Naomi just been threatened, even though she gave every indication of simply spending a quiet evening at home? If she hadn't, telling her about the stranger on her block would only have added to her anxiety. But Liz had phoned Chief Houghton, and he'd agreed to check on her. "I'll have Dixon keep a watch overnight," he'd promised. With that reassurance, she had been able to sleep after leaving Naomi.

After they had driven in silence for several minutes, Sadie cleared her throat noisily. "Now, you want to tell me what this little hike into Chicago is all about?"

Liz briefly related her adventure in the Sunrise Room and the bird-watcher's ire when he discovered her with the blueprint. "Beans tried to warn me he was coming, bless his canine heart, but it was too late. Felix just appeared there in the doorway, and he wasn't a bit happy about seeing me in his room." Liz recalled the man's eyes: the color of glacier ice and just as cold.

Sadie waited for the rest of the story.

"It was an old blueprint of a bird sanctuary. Dated eleven years back. I can't imagine why Felix would carry something like that around, especially on a vacation. It was titled 'Annabelle's Aviary.' Well, I got to thinking about some things Vera and Violet had said about Felix and his mother, Annabelle."

"And you think it has something to do with that man's death? Mr. O'Rourke or whatever his name really was." Sadie's brow wrinkled. "I thought the police had checked him out pretty thoroughly and written him off as a suspect—even if he was the one to find the body."

"The investigation has focused lately on that unidentified hitchhiker who was seen with O'Rourke—probably one of O'Rourke's associates from his prison days—but I don't think the chief has written off anyone. Jackson certainly hasn't." Liz paused, remembering his warning to question everything, that you never knew what might be important. "I guess I'm like him in that way. Neither of us takes anything for granted, and we both look beneath the surface of things—and people."

"You mean snooping," Sadie offered, but there was no rancor in her tone. Though she might never admit it, there was nothing Sadie loved more than probing into a good mystery. "So, you think the blueprint was for something Felix was building for his mother—or in her honor or something?"

Liz shrugged. Vera's odd comment resurfaced in her mind. *Felix and his mother never seemed to need anyone else but each other.* Then there was that bizarre tale about a deliberately ruined dress and flowers thrown down a well because Violet had collected them for Horner's mother.

But he was just a little boy, Violet had said. *We've quite forgiven him, haven't we?*

Vera's attitude indicated that she hadn't, but attitude was something Vera had in abundance.

"I understand that you're counting on Vera for her 'business expertise,'" Liz teased. "At least that's what she told us all when we were having breakfast the other day."

Sadie's harrumph sounded a lot like Vera's. "The woman's delusional," she said, "but she has offered a few sound suggestions here and there when it comes to display and organization. I'll have to give her that." She made an ironic face. "And at least it gives her something to think about other than Violet's little dalliance with Stefan."

"Dalliance? There's a Victorian-sounding term worthy of Emily Dickinson." Liz grinned. "Violet can hardly wait for tonight's festive occasion. Good thing we got everything ready in advance."

"We?" Sadie repeated, her eyebrows rising into her hairline. "While you and that handsome Jackson Cross were gallivanting around the country the other day, the Material Girls were at the lodge, working our tails off. Good thing Vera gave us a helping hand. She tried to enlist the help of Cousin Felix, but as usual, he was off spying on some poor meadowlark."

Liz warmed to Sadie's good-natured banter as the trip drew to a close. The time had gone quickly. They drove into the city, and after a companionable silence, Liz asked, "Don't you think it's odd that Felix would randomly call up the Holmes sisters and want to join them for a bird-watching holiday in a cold Indiana winter?"

Sadie grimaced. "I think we've all agreed that Felix Horner is an odd duck—no pun intended." She paused, then added thoughtfully, "So he designed a birdhouse and named it for his dead mother. That's rather sweet in a cockeyed sort of way."

"Not a birdhouse—an entire aviary stretching over miles. Very elaborate."

"So what are we doing here?" Sadie inclined her head toward the imposing skyline.

"The architect's name was on the blueprint. I thought it might be worthwhile to have a chat with him. I know he's still around. I called, but I didn't want to state my business over the phone."

"But your timing, Liz. This is such a long trip, and with the auction only hours away . . ."

Liz couldn't explain the urgency she felt, but this was something that just couldn't wait. "I know," she agreed, "but it's always an adventure to see Chicago, isn't it?"

"Makes me glad I had smarts enough to settle in Pleasant Creek." Sadie grinned. "The traffic on this road is terrible. People weaving in and out of lanes like slithering snakes. I swear the same cars keep passing us up. I think they lose time rather than gain it by trying to get ahead."

Liz squinted into the rearview mirror, unnerved by Sadie's offhand comment. Was someone following them? Weaving in and out to keep them in view? The motorcycle incident flashed through her mind. But there was nothing unusual about the endless stream of cars zipping around her now, careening back into whatever lane seemed momentarily open. And there were no black motorcycles. *Get a grip, Liz. You can't get all paranoid every time you see a vehicle close to you. Or a neighborhood snoop running into the woods.*

They whizzed past one exit after another, listening to the GPS track their progress. Liz felt her pulse pick up when the mechanical voice intoned, "You are approaching your destination." What would they learn at Ellerton's architectural firm? What would it mean for them all?

The building was a neat, two-story brick structure, probably built in the 1970s. The brass plate on the door read "Ellerton and Ellerton, Inc." They entered a tasteful, modest reception area and were greeted by a petite, well-dressed woman in her fifties, who offered a professional smile.

Liz got right to the point. She had pondered how she would explain her interest in the old blueprint and hoped it would sound plausible enough. "We'd like to speak with someone about an aviary that was designed by this company."

The soft gray brows came together. "An aviary—you mean some kind of bird zoo?"

"Yes," Liz said hopefully. "It was probably commissioned some ten or twelve years ago. I'm handling some business for a friend. The only name on the blueprint was 'Ellerton.' I wondered if the architect who drew it is still working here."

"This company is owned by Charles Ellerton. He and his son-in-law, J. Barrington, are the only two architects here. We are a small business, Miss . . ."

"Eckardt. Elizabeth Eckardt," Liz filled in. "And this is Sadie Schwarzentruber. We're from Pleasant Creek, Indiana. I own the Olde Mansion Inn there."

"Oh yes. A lovely spot—right there in Amish country," the receptionist said, her quick brown eyes lighting up. "I haven't been a guest there, but I've seen the photos on your website. A friend of mine stayed there once—said she had a very good experience."

"I'm so glad," Liz said, delighted that they had quickly found something in common.

"Why don't you have a seat over there and I'll find out if Mr. Ellerton can see you." She gestured to brown leather chairs arranged around a low table that held a variety of magazines. "May I bring you a cup of coffee?"

"Oh no. We're fine," Liz said, as the receptionist disappeared down a short hall, assuring them she would be right back.

"I hope the wait won't be too long," Sadie said when the receptionist was out of earshot. "Things get underway promptly at four. While everything's been set up at the lodge, there are always last-minute details to tend to."

"I'm aiming to get back well before then. That will give us plenty of time to dress and handle any problems that may arise."

Sadie nodded her head in guarded approval. "Let's just hope this isn't a wild goose chase and that we don't have a flat tire or run into some other problem on the way back."

"It may not prove anything or provide us with answers that will help Naomi, but we have to follow every lead." What they were following now was only a suspicion—a hunch that Felix might know more about what happened to Shane O'Rourke than he was saying. That morning when she'd left to pick up Sadie, she had been surprised to encounter him heading out in full bird-watching gear.

"My, we're up early," Felix had said, fixing her with a quirky smile that didn't quite reach his eyes. "You change your mind about coming along?" He fingered the binoculars on his chest.

"Oh no, but thank you, Felix," she had said nervously, imagining that he could divine her intention to look up the architectural firm. "I have other business to attend to. But I'll be back later. Today is the big quilt auction and dance at the Order of the Otter Lodge. Everyone will be there—well, at least I hope so." She had looked away uncomfortably from his intrusive glare. "Your cousins have worked hard to help us. I hope you'll come too—to show your support for the children's hospital." And she had walked on to her car, aware of his eyes fixed on her back.

When the receptionist returned, she was followed by a tall, slightly stooped gentleman with thinning silver hair and rimless glasses perched on a beak of a nose. A gray suit coat hung unbuttoned from narrow shoulders, as though he'd quickly thrown it on to greet his visitors.

"These ladies have come all the way from Pleasant Creek, Indiana, to see you," the receptionist said by way of introduction. "Miss Eckardt has a question about a blueprint developed here at Ellerton, Inc."

Weathered blue eyes took them in quickly, and a smile gentled the lined face. He bowed ceremoniously. "Please, come to my office," he said, turning. Over his shoulder he asked, "Has Margie offered you coffee?"

"Yes, but we're fine. Thank you for seeing us. We won't take much of your time."

It was a large working office with a drafting table set up by a window where the thin February sun eased in. "Please, sit down," Mr. Ellerton said, indicating two chairs near a desk adjacent to the drafting table.

"My son uses a sophisticated computer program, but I'm from the old school." He drew the rolling chair away from the cluttered table and sat facing them, blue-veined hands clasped over his bony knees. He looked at them expectantly.

Liking the aging architect's open face and respectful demeanor, Liz launched into her spiel. "I am handling some business matters for a friend and came across a blueprint with your name on it."

"Do you have it with you?"

It was a reasonable request; he was sure to wonder why she hadn't brought it. "No, I don't have it with me, but it's very distinctive. It looks like a bird sanctuary—quite large and intricate. I'm wondering if the aviary was actually built and, if so, where it might be located."

"An aviary," he repeated, tapping long fingers on his knees. He fixed interested eyes on Liz. "In all my years, I've only designed one. It was quite a challenge. Nothing at all like drawing plans for a house or business. Especially if you don't know much about enclosures for animals—especially animals that aren't usually 'cooped up.'" He smiled at his own witticism, then lifted a silvery eyebrow. "Mr. Horner, however, knew precisely what he wanted and spared no detail."

Liz felt her pulse racing. "Yes. Felix is nothing if not exact." She waited a few seconds before pressing. "Where was the aviary built, Mr. Ellerton?"

"It wasn't," he said simply. He shook his head. "Sad situation."

Liz waited, giving the architect time to recall what had happened more than a decade ago.

"I felt bad for the man. He really had his heart set on that project—wanted to dedicate it to his mother. Don't recall her name . . ."

"Annabelle?"

"Yes, that's it. Annabelle's Aviary. A clever alliteration. Felix was a clever man."

"What happened to the project?" Liz asked quietly.

"I don't really know exactly, Miss Eckardt," Ellerton said, frowning. "But Mr. Horner claimed he was the victim of a real estate scam. The property he had been purchasing for the aviary was sold out from under him by some developer. He lost everything. It was a terrible blow."

Something pinged in the back of Liz's mind. O'Rourke had been in real estate prior to his prison sentence. She leaned forward in her chair. "Do you happen to know the name of the developer who swindled him?"

"Sorry, I don't. There was a brief, nasty scandal about it, but it blew over. In the larger scheme of land development in this city, Horner's case was forgotten. I doubt it even made the papers." Ellerton breathed a long sigh, then straightened suddenly and slapped his knees, signaling that he'd come to the end of the interview and wanted to get back to his work. "Sorry I couldn't be more help."

Liz locked eyes with Sadie. Was it possible that O'Rourke was the one who had cheated Felix out of his life's dream? Had Felix somehow known his old nemesis would come to Pleasant Creek? Had he lain in wait for him and carried out his vengeance on the hapless swindler?

Given the right provocation, anyone could commit murder.

18

Guests were gradually gathering at the Order of the Otter Lodge for the quilt auction that would soon get underway. The balmy weather with which the day had started was holding. Liz sent up a prayer of thanks for the clear February day and exulted in the air of excitement that permeated the lodge.

She smoothed the folds of her red sheath dress and brushed back a strand of hair as she pulled bid cards from beneath a table by the door. The Material Girls had arrived and were bustling about the hall, intent on their particular assignments. Caitlyn and Opal were setting up a table where the lucky bidders would later pay for their purchases. Little Madison Ruby, ensconced on Opal's lap, would likely charm guests with her adorable grin and wide-eyed curiosity.

Liz had persuaded Sadie to conduct the auction herself rather than draw in a professional auctioneer. She was certain of Sadie's ability to describe each product with frankness and flair, and she knew how the community respected and admired Sew Welcome's grand lady. "No one knows these quilts better than you," Liz told her as she headed toward the kitchen where Mary Ann and her crew of volunteers were organizing the refreshments to be served later. Naomi was there too.

Naomi had asked to help in the kitchen rather than mingle with the crowd in the outer hall. She hadn't changed her mind about that, even after hearing the astonishing, long-anticipated news that an arrest had been made in the death of Shane O'Rourke.

Liz had been almost home with Sadie from their quick trip to Chicago when the beep of her cell phone indicated a waiting text. It was from Jackson. Her first thought was that something had come up, and that he was making apologies for not being able to attend the hospital charity event. She'd been surprised at the depth of her premature disappointment.

But when she had glanced down, disappointment gave way to glad relief. Jackson's brief message read, "Police have found mystery man. See you tonight."

"Sadie! They've found him!" Jackson's message was a more welcome sight than Liz could have imagined. "Thank God! I can't wait to tell Naomi." She hadn't waited but pulled off the road to forward the good news to her friend. They had decided to keep the information among the four of them for the time being—at least until they were assured the arrest would stick.

Now she was about to enjoy a fun event with her friends, and she felt lighter than air. She stepped out of the kitchen into the spacious lodge hall. The red-and-white garlands looked spectacular—thanks to Naomi, Liz, and a little help from the Internet. The candle centerpieces were ready to light when darkness fell. Stefan and two other helpers were setting up more chairs as the crowd grew. Kiera and Sarah stood at the door, greeting guests and directing traffic. The Holmes sisters assisted Sadie, seeing that each quilt entry was draped just right on the racks that Jackson had designed especially for the occasion.

Liz glanced around for Felix. He had agreed to take pictures during the event, but he hadn't yet arrived. Perhaps he had one more chickadee to capture with his fancy Nikon before heading to the lodge.

Suddenly, Sadie caught her eye from across the room and made a beeline for her. "I've forgotten Cora Hostettler's quilt," she whispered into Liz's ear. "She brought it into the shop the other day just as I was leaving, and I stashed it under the counter instead of putting it with the others. I could shoot myself!"

"Well, don't do that," Liz said, laughing. "Who'd auction off these quilts?"

Sadie pulled anxiously on her earlobe, eyes flashing. "Ain't funny. We need that quilt. It's the only Double Wedding Ring in the show."

"Not to worry," Liz said. "It won't take but a few minutes for me to run back and get it. You go ahead and start the auction. I'll be back with Cora's Wedding Ring long before you spin through all those quilts."

She grabbed her jacket from the coat rack reserved for kitchen workers. When she saw Naomi's coat hanging next to hers, she made a quick decision to ask her friend to come along. Naomi was still nervous and vulnerable, and likely would be until confirmation of the mystery man's guilt was made public. She had been through a lot since the investigation began, not the least of which were the whispers and anonymous calls. Liz wanted to stay close to her.

"You okay?" she asked Naomi when they were inside the Acura and headed toward the inn.

"I'm fine," she said quickly but without the enthusiasm Liz was hoping for.

She'll be back to her old self once this is finally cleared up, she thought. *For now, we'll keep her mind occupied with the day's events.* "Sadie forgot to bring Cora Hostettler's quilt," she said. "We'll just run in and pick it up."

Naomi merely nodded.

She pulled around to the back of the inn and parked the car near the patio entrance. "Let's go through the utility room. The quilt's probably in a humongous box; I'll need your help."

She was surprised to see a car parked behind the inn, a car that looked very much like the one that belonged to Felix Horner. Likely he was preparing to leave for the lodge, but why was he exiting from the rear of the inn? Guests never used that door.

As she turned the key in the lock she was startled to hear a shuffling noise coming from inside the utility room. *It couldn't be Stefan; I left him at the lodge setting up chairs. Maybe it's Rachel; she was waiting for her mother so they could go to the quilt auction together.* The noise stopped abruptly. She swung the door open and came face to face with Felix Horner, the flaps of his hunter's cap dangling at his shoulders.

She flipped the light switch, and his magnified eyes widened even further. He was dressed for the outdoors, holding a suitcase in one hand and a portfolio in the other. Binoculars and camera cases hung around his neck. Ashen-faced, he stuttered, "You! I was just—that is, I—"

Liz stared. "Surely you're not leaving."

Two bright spots appeared on the little man's cheeks, and his eyes darkened beneath the thick brows. His jaw twitched as though he was clenching his teeth. "Get out of my way," he demanded, angling away from the two women.

Liz, with Naomi close behind her, moved to block his passage. "But you know that Chief Houghton said that no one is allowed to leave town yet." She peered at him through narrowed eyes. "Especially without paying the bill," she added meaningfully.

Suddenly, something silver flashed in the air. Liz felt her heart stop at the sight of the pistol Felix drew from his jacket pocket. Absurdly, her eyes focused on the fine red hairs covering his hands. Behind her, Naomi gasped.

Heart pounding, Liz lifted her hands and drew back, bumping into Naomi. "So," she said when she could catch her breath, "pictures *aren't* the only thing you shoot!"

"This is what comes of all your snooping," he said, waving the gun menacingly and making a doleful clucking noise with his tongue. "You couldn't leave it alone, couldn't mind your own business."

Liz squared her shoulders and prayed for calm. "What are you talking about?"

"I had you followed to Ellerton's office. I know you were prying into my affairs. So now you know what that swindler Winston did." Wet lips protruded in a childish pout that might have been funny if it wasn't so abundantly clear that Felix Horner was a dangerous man.

So it was Winston who had spoiled Horner's dream for a bird sanctuary. Stunned, she stared at Felix, remembering the strength and agility he had displayed shinnying down a tree. She thought of the furtive cell phone calls. She had only casually wondered what business the bird-watcher might have, never imagining that he might be contacting a partner. Then there were the twins' clues, which she had not taken seriously until now. She stared at his hand—a hand that had shot a man he despised. *Dear God!*

"It was you!" Naomi stammered, pulling around Liz as though she would lunge at Felix. "You killed him!"

"Stay back!" Felix ordered, eyes bulging behind his glasses. "Both of you." He wiped sweat from his forehead and peered anxiously through the open utility door where Liz's car idled.

Was he expecting someone? The person who had followed them into Chicago perhaps? Sadie had been right about seeing a car pass them and fall back several times. Could it be the same person she and Jackson had seen in Felix's car near the abandoned barn?

"You won't get far," Liz said tauntingly. "The police picked up your partner. He's probably telling the chief all about you right now."

The glacier-like eyes seemed to freeze momentarily, then began to flash back and forth. *He must have known his partner had been caught. Isn't that why he's skipping out?*

Felix stamped his left foot like a spoiled child. An expletive fell from the curt lips. "Why couldn't he just do what he was told?"

"Who?"

Indifferent to her question, he continued his rant. "All he had to do was follow Winston and lead me to him. Then he was supposed to clear out. The idiot! I paid him good money—but it wasn't enough for him." He glared straight at Naomi. "We would be home free—but he had to wring money out of you too! I told him to just get out of town since everyone already believed you were guilty." He waved the gun at Naomi.

Liz struggled to make sense of the words she was hearing. She glanced at Naomi's face and saw that it was white as a sheet. She glared back at Felix. "You killed him and let Naomi take the blame?" She took a step toward him. "You said you hated guns," she accused. "Where did you hide the gun you used to shoot Mr. O'Rourke?"

"Mr. O'Rourke!" Felix repeated with a sneer. "He was no mister; he was a conniving skunk. Well, I showed him." He paused, his eyes glittery as though harking back to the moment with twisted pleasure. "Mind you, he never saw it coming—and as for the ineptitude of your local police, they could have dragged that lake until doomsday and they'd never have found it."

Liz could see he was enjoying his triumph. She took a chance at goading him further, in spite of the pistol waving dangerously in their direction. "So you didn't throw it in the lake."

"That would have been too easy. Even in winter, the police would have found it. It took me a little while to search out the tree well in advance—the tree with just the right hollow. Later, I went back for it—as you can see."

Liz gasped. The smug smile on his lips froze her bones. He had disposed of the gun after shooting O'Rourke, then calmly called 911 to say he'd found a body in the snow. He'd been so believable—there was nothing to give him away, except perhaps those cold, colorless eyes. She steadied herself and said calmly, "You can't possibly hope to get away with murder. They've caught your spying friend, and they'll be coming for you. You've sealed your own doom."

"Shut up!" Felix ordered through gritted teeth. "Now, we're all going back outside. Slowly." He leveled the gun in their faces. "Get in the car. You're going to drive," he ordered Liz. "And you . . ." he said, turning his icy gaze on Naomi. "Get in the front with her. I'm going to be right behind you with a gun pointed at your pretty heads, so don't try anything."

19

"We're going for a little ride, ladies. Head out of town and take the county road. Then turn north," Felix ordered. Almost as an afterthought, he added, "I'll take those purses."

Liz handed over hers, and Naomi followed suit. They were not going to be able to call anyone, even if an opportunity presented itself. She scanned the landscape, seeing not a single soul who might witness what was happening. With most of the town at the auction, how could she alert someone to their plight? "Where are you taking us?" she demanded.

"Never mind. Just do what I tell you."

She put the Acura in gear and drove toward the county road, her fingers trembling as she gripped the steering wheel. Without looking at her, she could see Naomi shaking her head and hear her swallowing hard. "I'm sorry. I'm so sorry," she moaned just above a whisper.

Three cars passed by, and then they were alone on the road. It was a familiar road—the one she and Naomi took to the Serenity Arms Residence. She shivered, realizing that the sun would be setting very soon. It would be dark, and no one knew where they were. *Where is he taking us? What does he plan to do with us?* She shuddered as grim possibilities flashed through her mind.

Suddenly a horse and buggy appeared on the horizon. The black-hatted, bearded driver who held the reins was coming toward them at a sedate trot. *Dear God, please let it be someone I know, someone who might help us!*

"Just keep your eyes on the road and drive at a steady pace. Don't get any funny ideas," Felix threatened.

In her mirror, Liz could see Felix crouch lower in the seat, trying to hide from the approaching Amish driver. What signal could she give the man that they were in trouble? She squinted in the gathering twilight, trying to make out the face, hoping to catch his eye and somehow communicate their distress, but the lone man in the buggy kept his shaded face forward, his body rigid on the plank seat.

"One sound from that mouth of yours, and it will be the last one you make," Felix hissed.

The Amish man would soon pass them by, unaware of what was happening inside the English car. *Why doesn't he look at me?* Suddenly, Liz knew the identity of the tall man in black hat and beard. *Ephraim Hausen!* She fixed her eyes on his face, her mind screaming for him to stop. *Do something!* But he simply passed them by, probably heading home to his farm. He hadn't given them the slightest glance, let alone a wave of greeting or any sign that they had met on the country road. Beside her, Naomi moaned, her voice a muted wail of despair.

When the buggy was gone, Felix straightened up in the seat and waved the gun in a threatening arc. "Very wise, Miss Eckardt," he said. "Now step on it!" They drove on in silence until he barked, "Take that road there—the next left turn."

It was a private road, winding, full of ruts and gravel, and bordered by scraggly evergreens. "But there's nothing on that road," Liz began to protest. "Just an abandoned barn." Then she realized that the lopsided, weathered old outbuilding shrouded by overgrown bushes and scrub pine was exactly where Felix was taking them. *A perfect place to hide out or to . . .* Her mind refused to finish the thought.

"Keep going," he demanded, leaning forward, the gun still poised in his hand. As his tension rose, his voice became squeaky and alarming.

"Pull through that maze of bushes and go around to the rear." Sarcastically, he added, "Too bad about the scratches on your pretty car."

When the car was camouflaged from the road, Felix herded Liz and Naomi inside the gloomy barn that smelled like musty straw and rotting wood. Hundreds of cobwebs clung to rafters and stalls. The sticky stuff draped their faces as they were goaded forward amid abandoned pails and rusted tools that littered the floor. In one corner, something was partially concealed by a moldy tarp. A tractor? Some other farm implement? With sudden clarity she knew what it was. A motorcycle—eerily like the one that had harassed her and Naomi on the road from Serenity Arms. The old abandoned barn had been the mystery man's hideout.

"Keep moving. Over there." Felix pushed the hard muzzle of the gun into her back.

She nearly tripped over a concrete slab upon which lay the remains of a wood fire. Cluttered around it were empty bottles and plastic foam containers. Someone had been living here, keeping warm on cold February nights. Though the rafters above the slab allowed for ventilation, the old barn was a tinderbox. One stray spark could have burned it to the ground!

Felix urged them toward the loft and told them to climb up the ladder. "I'm watching your every move," he warned and clambered briskly after them. "Sit down by those posts. Both of you."

Through a small, wire-meshed window above them, dusk was beginning to fall. Was anyone looking for them? "What are you going to do?" Liz asked, hating the tremor in her voice.

Felix grabbed a dirty rope coiled in the straw and tied their wrists to the thick wooden beams—Liz first and then Naomi. Liz could smell a mix of onions and sweat as he leaned over her and yanked the rope tight. He inspected his work and backed down from the loft, taking a place below where he could keep an eye on them from a distance.

"It's all my fault," Naomi whispered. "But I didn't know he had anything to do with killing Trevor. He kept saying he knew I had done it and that we both should be glad he was dead." She wiped fresh tears from her streaked face. "Then he said I had to give him the money that Trevor originally demanded."

"Felix's partner was trying to blackmail you?" Liz asked, incredulous. "Why, Naomi? What's this all about?"

She lowered her head, and her hair veiled her face. "He—he threatened my mother. He said unless I gave him the money he would tell her about Willie John." She took a choking breath. "Trevor must have told him."

"Told him what?" Liz asked breathlessly.

"Willie John was no war hero. He was actually dishonorably discharged and died shortly afterward in an automobile accident. We were able to keep the news out of the papers in the beginning, but when the scandal broke, Mother had a breakdown that eventually became dementia. She grew steadily worse. I had to get her away. That's why I left Maine and came to Indiana. I thought she was safe—that we were all safe from the awful truth. That was years ago, but somehow Trevor found out." She swallowed hard. "If Mother ever remembered the truth, it would kill her. She was—is—so proud of her son."

"Oh, Naomi," Liz breathed.

Naomi squeezed back tears. "Trevor showed up here in Pleasant Creek, demanding money to keep our family secret. I arranged to get it, but the next day he turned up dead." Her voice dwindled to a whisper. "I thought it was all over, but . . ."

Liz glanced at Felix restlessly pacing the rough floor below, apparently planning his next move. Liz shivered. He had committed murder and kidnapped two women. He didn't have a lot to lose.

Naomi shook her head despondently and went on. "I could hardly believe it when this man I don't even know came to my house saying he knew all about the scandal and how Willie John actually died. He said he knew I had killed Trevor and that if I knew what was good for me, I'd give him twenty thousand dollars."

"Did you give it to him?"

"I gave him my mother's ring and all the money I could scrape together without going to the bank." Naomi lowered her head. "I couldn't go to the bank. The police already think I killed Trevor."

Liz was starting to make sense of everything that had followed. Felix had paid his partner to pinpoint Winston and killed Winston out of revenge. Then his partner, learning of the family scandal from a boastful Trevor, had schemed to blackmail Naomi. *A mystery wrapped in an enigma*, Liz thought. *No wonder this whole case has had everyone stymied.*

"I'm so sorry," Naomi lamented again. "Look what I've done! I've put you in terrible danger."

Felix, suitcase and portfolio in hand, suddenly stopped pacing and crossed over to the ladder. He looked up to the loft and dangled Liz's car keys from an index finger. "I'm afraid I'll have to leave you now," he said and pressed his lips together.

"You're going to steal my car?" Liz said. "And leave us here? It's getting dark and it will be cold." She could see that his forehead was bathed in sweat and that his face was practically glowing red. *Can I appeal to his better nature?* she wondered. *Does he have one?* "Don't make things worse by doing this," she urged. "You know this isn't right."

He shuffled his feet and seemed to hesitate, then spoke decisively. "Winston deserved to die—after what he did to my mother and to hundreds of defenseless birds who needed a home. It was only right."

"There was nothing right about what you did," Liz charged recklessly. "It was just plain murder!"

He stamped his left foot petulantly again and jutted his chin out as the muscles in his temples twitched. Turning his back to her, he paced angrily for a while before spinning around and returning to stand under the loft. He stared up at Liz. "It's your fault. Mind you, I had no quarrel with either of you ladies until you got in my way." He sniffed, and the thick spectacles bobbed on his nose.

Liz began to protest anew when suddenly there was a loud noise at the window just above her head.

"What's *that*?" Felix shouted and began scrambling up the ladder. "What are you—"

Liz stared openmouthed at a mourning dove flapping its wings helplessly against the window. Somehow it had gotten trapped between the wire mesh and the window and couldn't extricate itself. Its usual soft cooing became a high-pitched frantic wail as it beat against the smudged glass.

Felix lunged toward the window with a cry of his own, forgetting the pistol that fell from his hand. "We've got to help it! It'll die in there!"

Liz kept her eyes on Felix but stretched her leg as far as she could and kicked the gun to the floor below. It clattered sharply against the concrete slab in the middle of the barn.

Felix jerked around, his face an angry red mask. "You shouldn't have done that!" he shrieked. But unbelievably, instead of racing down to retrieve the gun, he began climbing up the rafters. As he inched upward, he made incoherent soothing noises to the thrashing bird.

Liz struggled against the rope and watched Felix with amazement. He had shot an unarmed man and kidnapped two women, but all of that was forgotten in his fervor to rescue a trapped bird.

Felix scrambled over the crossbeam and yanked at the window in a frantic effort to raise it. It was shut tight, and he couldn't budge it. "I'll have to break the glass," he continued speaking to the dove, "but don't you worry. I'll get you out."

With his elbow, he smashed the glass, sending shards spraying everywhere. He continued to pound against the thick mesh until, with a throttled cry, the bird was free and surged to the sky. "You're all right now," Felix soothed. "You're all right. . ."

Suddenly the barn door flew open. Bursts of light flared, momentarily blinding them. "Liz!" someone called.

At the sound of the familiar voice, relief washed over her. "Up here!" she yelled as Jackson raced inside, followed by Chief Houghton and another policeman. "The gun's down there," she shouted, bobbing her head in the direction she had kicked it.

The chief headed for the gun, but Jackson was up the ladder and advancing on Felix Horner with his hands balled into fists. He quickly had him detained and trundled him down to the main floor where he was cuffed and led out of the barn.

Liz felt her heart leap as Jackson scrambled back up to the loft and knelt to cut the ropes away. She flung her stiff arms around his neck and felt his arms encircle her. "How did you find me? How did you know?" she cried with relief.

But he didn't answer—not in words, but she would always remember his gentle murmurs mingled with the wonderful woodsy fragrance of him.

20

When Liz and Naomi entered with Jackson, the Otter Lodge hall resounded with happy chatter and music from a small ensemble. The auction long over, the floor had been cleared for dancing, and tables were set around the perimeter with red-and-white cloths and the candle centerpieces Liz and Naomi had prepared.

Sadie gave them no time to take off their coats but flung her arms out to engulf first Liz and then Naomi. "Thank God!" she said over and over, and then she pulled back to look into their faces. "Are you all right? We were worried sick about you!" She turned her frantic glance to Jackson. "Thank God you found them, but where were they? How did you find them?"

"It's Rachel we can thank," Jackson said quietly. "Rachel—and Ephraim."

"Ephraim!" Sadie repeated, aghast. "Now I know I'm not hearing right. But for heaven's sake, get on in here; we have a table reserved for you—with all of us. And we want to hear all about it. Land sakes, when you didn't show up, we couldn't imagine what had happened. We kept the auction going until every quilt was sold, and then the floor was cleared for the party and you still weren't here." Sadie took Liz by one arm and Naomi by the other and trundled them through the crowd.

Liz brushed straw from her winter coat and hoped no one would notice her dusty shoes and the railroad-track run in her hose. They hadn't taken off their coats the whole time they were at the mercy of Felix Horner, so her good red dress was just possibly still presentable.

But she was so glad to be safe among friends with Jackson close by, that she didn't care about how she looked.

"Are you sure you don't want to go home?" Jackson had asked when they were safely inside his car and their captor was being hauled away. He had grilled her while still in the barn: Could she walk? Was she hurt? Could he do anything? She had read the mix of anger and relief in his eyes as Felix was led out to the squad car. Liz and Naomi would have to give full statements in the morning, but Chief Houghton had left them in Jackson's care for the night.

"We've looked forward to this for so long," Liz had told him ardently, trying to smooth her tangled hair. "I want to go to the party—what's left of it—even though I may look like something the cat dragged in."

"You look beautiful," Jackson had said with conviction. He'd helped them gently into his car and taken them to the lodge. Now the table at the south end of the hall was encircled by the Material Girls, who eagerly watched them approach. Mary Ann had tears in her eyes, and Caitlyn was practically dancing in place with excitement. Little Madison Ruby had been confined to her high chair so that Grandma Opal's arms were free to welcome her friends.

Rachel stood off to one side, away from the great round table where the Material Girls were waiting. She clasped her arms around herself as though she was cold in her pink A-line dress, her soft blonde hair coiled around her shoulders. Liz gestured for her to join them; she would let Rachel tell her own story to the detail-hungry group of friends.

"I was at the inn," she said, directing her comments to Liz. "Upstairs in my room. I saw you drive up and come inside, but you didn't go back out, so I went to investigate. I checked the shop and all the rooms on the lower level before I thought of going to the utility room." She shuddered and swallowed before continuing. "I saw that Mr. Horner pushing you into your car, and I saw the gun he was holding."

Caitlyn let out a gasp. "What did you do?"

"I was so stunned I didn't know what to do. But I knew I had to tell somebody, to get help." Rachel's eyes flashed. "I got in my car but it wouldn't start, no matter what I did. My old cell phone had stopped working too, so I ran home to Mutter. Vater was just coming home in the buggy. I was so afraid he wouldn't help me. He didn't even want me in the house." She lowered her eyes briefly, perhaps in shame, then turned to Liz. "But when he heard that you were in trouble, he told me to get in the buggy."

Jackson broke in, hazel eyes trained on Liz. "Ephraim had passed you in his buggy on the old Post Road that leads to the abandoned barn on his way home. When Rachel told her parents what she'd seen, he started for town with Rachel—or maybe to the Borkholder farm where there's a phone in the barn—but then they saw me heading toward the inn. Sadie had phoned to tell me something was wrong, that it shouldn't have taken you so long to get the quilt you'd gone after."

"That's how you guessed we were in the old barn!" Liz said. "Thank God you came!" She shook her head with wonder. *And to think that it was Ephraim, of all people, who had helped to rescue us.*

"After Rachel told me what she'd seen, I put in a quick call to Houghton," Jackson finished. "Long story short, our not-so-friendly bird-watcher is in custody, along with his partner."

"But why did he do it?" Mary Ann asked incredulously.

Liz recounted the saga of Felix Horner's bitter revenge and the bird sanctuary that was never built. "He hired O'Rourke's former cellmate to find him. The would-be bounty hunter tracked O'Rourke to Pleasant

Creek and learned of O'Rourke's plan to blackmail Naomi, and then when O'Rourke was killed, the man Felix hired as his spy took over and demanded money to keep her family secret."

Beside her, Naomi spoke quietly. "I was so afraid for my mother. It was him in her room that day pretending to be a chaplain." She looked at Liz sitting on her left. "He could have . . ." She stopped and leaned forward to rest her elbows on the table and clapped her hands to her temples. "I should have told the police everything. I'm so sorry for the trouble I caused."

Liz put a hand on Naomi's shoulder. "Felix is the one at fault. His anger and bitterness made him lose all perspective of what is good and right." There would be much more to unpack about this many-layered mystery, but it had been a long and trying day. She was tired—and hungry.

"I think that's enough questions." Sadie broke in sternly. "Our friends are safe, and the bad guys are locked up. Time to enjoy the party!" She headed toward the table where Vera and Violet were chatting with some of Sew Welcome's regulars.

Liz had an idea that the Holmes twins would not be all that surprised to learn what their cousin had been up to. Vera's distaste for him had been warranted. As for Violet, she would mourn over Felix, but she'd no doubt be consoled by Stefan who was looking very debonair in his dark blue suit and crimson tie. A return visit to the Olde Mansion Inn at some future date—at least by Violet—seemed very likely. Liz would make sure she found a few odd jobs for Stefan to do when that happened.

Mary Ann commandeered Rachel and Naomi to fetch food and fresh drinks from the kitchen. Caitlyn struck up a conversation with a sandy-haired doctor at the next table, and Opal went to rescue Madison Ruby, leaving Liz and Jackson temporarily by themselves.

Liz released a long sigh and turned to Jackson. "I'm so glad it's over. Well, almost over. I'm especially happy for Naomi. She's been through an awful ordeal."

"The chief said they found the blackmail money and Moriah's ring in his partner's motorcycle saddlebag," Jackson said. "The guy was supposed to be working for Felix but he was playing both sides of the fence."

"You were suspicious of Felix from the beginning, weren't you?" Liz asked.

He leaned back in his chair and regarded her thoughtfully. "I was suspicious of everybody—just like you were. But you were the one who figured out the connection between Horner and the victim." He shook his head from side to side. "When I think of you in the same house with that man . . ." The words fell away as he looked deeply into her eyes, tenderness in his own.

The music wrapped around them, compelling and sweet, and when the slow strains of *The Rose* began, they both fell silent. Jackson stood and held out his hand. "The dance you promised to save me—I think this is the one."

Up to this point, we've been doing all the writing. Now it's *your* turn!

Tell us what you think about this book, the characters, the bad guy, or anything else you'd like to share with us about this series. We can't wait to hear from *you*!

Log on to give us your feedback at:
https://www.surveymonkey.com/r/AmishInn

Annie's® FICTION

Learn more about Annie's fiction books at

AnniesFiction.com

We've designed the Annie's Fiction website especially for you!

Access your e-books • Read sample chapters • Manage your account

Choose from one of these great series:

Amish Inn Mysteries

Annie's Attic Mysteries

Annie's Mysteries Unraveled

Annie's Quilted Mysteries

Annie's Secrets of the Quilt

Annie's Sweet Intrigue

Antique Shop Mysteries

Chocolate Shoppe Mysteries

Creative Woman Mysteries

Hearts of Amish Country

Inn at Magnolia Harbor

Secrets of the Castleton Manor Library

Scottish Bakehouse Mysteries

Victorian Mansion Flower Shop Mysteries

What are you waiting for? Visit us now at **AnniesFiction.com!**